Also by Ken Olive

Goldie's Garden

Special Corps

Snap Justice

Publisher: Ken Olive Publishing

ISBN-13: 978-0-615-49931-4
ISBN-10: 0-615-49931-7

First Edition: July 2011

10 9 8 7 6 5 4 3 2 1

The Killing Tour

By

Ken Olive

Foreword

An individual's actions are comprised of four basic elements. *Background*, *Training*, *Situation*, and *Inclination*.

How and where one is born, and grows, is *Background*. The way the seed is planted, the environment around it. The beginning of the journey. Is he born into a culture racked by hunger and disease, or one which affords abundant food and modern medicine?

The way this *Background* is further cultivated and directed, is *Training*. Is he grown like the orchid? Fragile, singular, and delicately? Or is he treated with neglect or abuse, as with the dandelion, or crabgrass, and grown conditioned to withstand harsh surroundings and cruel climates?

Situation, is what all of us encounter hundreds of times each and every day of our existence. Left or right, in the fork of the road ahead? Extra crispy, or hot and spicy? Regular or de-cafe? Decisions, which put us on a specific path, throughout our life's journey.

Inclination, the final element, is how one responds to sudden, or opportunistic situations. The basic animal instinct of "fight or flight?" is the best example of this predisposition. It is a trigger, if you will, which lies deep in the reptilian recesses of our brain. Our thinking patterns evolved over millions of years, building reason, restraint, and rational processes over this primitive beginning of a brain, but the reptilian part is still there.

The Killing Tour

Today, rational thought, and the consequences of our actions, usually triumph over that ancient survival center located near the top of the brain stem.

But there are constant struggles. Battles between rational thought and extreme behavior.

The third element, *Situation*, is simply a series of decisions leading to a particular path.

Hence, the final action, *Inclination*, how the person responds to the other three elements.

This the story you are about to read.

To attempt to explain it, is fruitless. To understand it, can only be accomplished by the being, itself.

Man is a combination of good and evil. Each of us must make our own determination and decisions.

Book One

The Killing Tour

Chapter One

Travis Bayne walked, this time headed west. It was fall. The day had begun with that special crispness in the air, but had soon surrendered to the sun's heat before noon. He had worn this pair of army-issued jump boots for so many miles they felt like athletic shoes. Nike or some other athletic brand was supposed to be the best. Travis Bayne didn't care. He wasn't tuned in to the small, unimportant things in the world.

He had been through lots of boots, bought at surplus stores, and had travelled thousands of miles. For Travis, it was him and the road. He had walked and hitched across the country too many times to count in the past few years.

His wore a western straw hat sat cocked forward over his tanned face. He still retained that boyish look he had been blessed with.

The oversized Army backpack he wore was his constant companion. The pack was heavy, but his posture was perfectly upright. Travis took great pride in doing things the correct way. This wasn't the U.S. Army Special Forces, Delta Squad, anymore, but he was still a proper soldier.

He wasn't huge, but large enough at 6'3," and Travis was in great muscular shape. Even jump school training had been easy for him at Ft. Benning, where they usually "washed out" 70% of the applicants. Travis had been blessed with a thick mane of hair, raven black, which he kept cut, a quarter-inch short, not much more than a "buzz." He was boyishly handsome, and used that to his advantage. Today was just another travel day. A day closer to his ending tour.

He was still fit because it was part of his routine. He did 200 push-ups and 400 sit-ups each morning. Getting soft was not an option for him. He always wanted to be ready. This, his final mission, was self directed. And as always, was he entirely alone, no back up. He had always worked in the shadows, and used deception.

When he was remembering his past, he usually had his "mean Travis" face on, his expression was baleful. It's demeanor telegraphed his essence perfectly. One quick glance left no doubt of the malevolence which had taken seed within this man, struggling for the chance to get out.

When Travis walked through a rural town, most men averted their eyes, then stared at his back. He could feel them doing it. Mothers would call their children inside, "come out of the yard," or "off the porch," they would yell. Mongrel dogs, even pit bulls, barked, but from a distance and with their tails tucked low between their legs. Travis sensed it, and liked it. It made him feel whole.

It was times like this, reliving his early childhood memories, when he let his "nice Travis" look be subjugated, and showed his true self. He started to remember things about his childhood...

"Travis...Travis Bayne," the woman screamed his name out the back door. "Come on in, Uncle Bob will be home soon, and he wants us all at the table ready to eat." He could remember her face. Gladys, or "Aunt Gladys," as she liked to be called, was his foster mother. His foster family's last name had been Monroe. Travis travelled even earlier, back to the beginning of his memory..

Travis had been dumped, left to fend for himself. He was abandoned on the steps of the North Raleigh Christian Orphanage, one cold night. He couldn't remember his birth parents, just that they left him there after a long drive. He sat on the orphanage stone steps, as instructed, holding a brown "Piggly Wiggly" grocery sack full of his clothes.

The next morning had been brought inside the building. Travis met the orphanage director, Mr. Jim O'Keefe, a pleasant, balding man. "Do you know where you live?" all the grown-ups asked. He would just shake his head and answer, "From place to place." All he knew was that his name was Travis Bayne, and he was 5 years old. What had he done wrong, he wondered?

Now he saw his past more clearly. In his cold mind's eye, there was "Aunt Gladys" standing on the porch, screaming his name. She and "Uncle Bob," were his third set of foster parents. They had been the evil ones, who helped shape him into what he had become.

His first foster parents were kind people. Their name was Martin. They had been good people, and he stayed with them the longest. Mr. Ted Martin was a hard worker. "He works for us, and the Lord," Ms. Martin would say. They had kept him well fed and sent him to school, for over 6 years. Then, late one afternoon, a North Carolina Highway Patrolman had rung the door bell.

With his hat in his hand, he told his foster Mom that his Foster Dad, Ted, had been killed in an accident at the lumber mill. Two months later, his surrogate Mom had caught the cancer, and it never let go. It was back to the orphanage for Travis. It wasn't right. It wasn't right at all. What did he do wrong? Travis cared about them.

Being older, it was harder to get taken into another home, but a few months later, another childless couple named Scott and Janice Richards, took a chance on Travis. They had been the best people he had lived with. They had taken him in, and raised him right, by all parental standards. They were a cute couple. She was blonde and pert, always smiling. He was shorter and stout, but very industrious, with an infectious laugh, which he used frequently.

They were both happy they finally had a "son," they had tried to have their own for years, but failed. Then God gave them Travis. It was a nice home, with several acres of working farm.

Travis was doing better. The melancholy had worn off from his first experience, and he was helping out with the farm chores, whether it be tending the hogs, or nailing up barbed wire. Once, Mr. Richards even let Travis drive the tractor. He loved being outside.

They liked Travis, and he liked them. On his thirteenth birthday, they had made a big deal out of him becoming a "man." They started talking about "adoption." Travis was constantly smiling.

As fate would have it, just before Travis reached fifteen, Mr. Richards had a severe stroke. For several months of rehabilitation Scott tried to learn to walk again, to talk, without slurring his words. He worked hard at this, too. Travis could feel it. His wife hired people to help with the farm, as she worked with her husband to make him whole again, without success.

The doctors said that his stroke had been too severe to expect even a partial recovery. Finally, after seeing the visiting doctors shake their collective heads, Mr. Richards gave up, and slid further from reality.

Even with the disability checks, and the $187 a month the state was paying Mrs. Richards for keeping Travis, she lost the farm to the bank. It was, as before, back to the orphanage for Travis. He was heartbroken. In his eyes he had failed, again. It was here, he met Lester.

After a few months, Travis was taken to the interview room where he met "Uncle Bob" and "Aunt Gladys, Monroe." They asked Travis if he wanted out of the orphanage, did he want to become part of a family. To all of this Travis nodded greedily, and kept his smiling face plastered on.

After his meeting with the Monroe's, he sat outside the room for what seemed to Travis, an eternity. Finally he looked up and saw Mr. O'Keefe walking his way. He had a smile on his face. Tears ran down Travis' face as he was told that the Monroes had been impressed. They would return to pick him up in three days. It took a day or two to get the paperwork done, and they wanted to get his room ready at his new "home."

Travis heard around the orphanage that this couple had a reputation. They were strictly foster parents for the state money, not just the kindness in their hearts. They had two other foster children, twin girls, and Travis would just be a "car payment" for the Monroes. But Travis was still a minor, at fifteen, a pretty large minor, but still someone who had no say about his life's direction.

Travis knew that at his age, he couldn't misbehave. In all likelihood, this would be his last chance to become part of a real family. If he "screwed up" this opportunity, he would be part of the "system" until he was eighteen, and put out on his own after that.

The day finally came. Travis had been on the top bunk bed staring out the window onto the street outside since sunrise. He was hoping the Monroes wouldn't change their mind, or forget about him. Just as soon as the "grandfather clock" in the foyer sounded 9 a.m., Bob and Gladys Monroe arrived in a blue Chevy Nova, to transport him to his new home. Travis was warm and happy again.

They drove, under skies which were "Carolina blue" for about half an hour to a small suburb named Macedonia, just south of Raleigh. Travis thought the name a little pompous, but Aunt Gladys was full of stories. She knew the town's history, and it's place in the "war against the northern aggression," as she called it. Gladys reminded him of a chicken with a long skinny neck and a narrow nose. She had a nervous tic, clearing her throat every ten seconds, or so. Travis stared at her at first, then decided it best to ignore the habit.

The Nova stopped in front of a white, two-story house up a steep hill. "We're here" Uncle Bob declared, and they drove up the rutted driveway, to the front porch. Sitting on the porch were two girls, obviously twins, maybe a year older or younger than Travis, who was now sixteen. They were cute, blonde, and from what limited TV Travis had been exposed to, the girls looked like cheerleaders.

Gladys introduced them as Cindi and Tammy Stone. Their parents, and a brother had been killed in a auto accident down in Cary, a few years ago. There had been people want to adopt one or the other, but the girls wanted to stay together. They'd lost their whole family one afternoon. They wouldn't split up now. But trying to place two, teenage girls had been difficult. Difficult at least until the Monroes came on the scene.

Gladys had told Travis earlier the girls had been part of the family for almost three years, now. They both politely rose to shake his hand, then helped him with his two bags of clothes, an old football, and a world globe which comprised the totality of his possessions. The bags were still from "Piggly Wiggly."

Two

The girls led him upstairs, and opened the door to a small bedroom containing a single bed, dresser, table, and mirror. It looked huge to Travis when compared to the orphanage, which had rows of beds. Tammy said, "Travis, this is your room. Go ahead and hang up your clothes, the dresser is empty, so you can store your folding things there. The bathroom is down the hall. You'll have to share it with us, though."

Cindi chipped in, "It's your room when you're good, that is." Tammy snapped at her sister, "There will be plenty of time for that stuff, later, and keep smiling, or else Bob will think we're talking about him." Travis was puzzled, but didn't ask any questions.

It was Sunday, and Uncle Bob asked Travis to go for a short walk with him around the property, "Just to get to know each other." They walked outside. Bob set a slow pace around the property. There was still plenty of heat in the afternoon sun.

Bob Monroe was a painter, by trade, and a farmer by hobby. His hobby helped provide extra food on the table. Bob was around 40 years old, lean, if not downright skinny.

He had thinning, brownish hair. He stood about 6 feet tall, and possessed a protruding Adam's apple, which bobbed up and down when he spoke. His left ear he kept covered with a comb-over from his hair. When the wind blew, Travis could see that it was a tiny, deformed stump of an ear, which Bob tried to keep hidden. Travis didn't stare. Bob was wearing jeans and a flannel shirt, both of which might have been too small for Travis, who was sixteen now.

He looked at Travis, "I heard you had some farming experience, that's why I took you in. I need some help around here. Nothing heavy, just tending to the animals and doin' a few repairs."

"I had a boy here who run off a few months ago. He was eighteen, had every right to do as he pleased, but didn't say thanks or nothin'. Came home from my job one day and the wife said he'd lit out no sooner than my painting truck was out of sight when I left that morning."

Bob just shook his head, "No gratitude. Not a word from that boy, and after the help we gave to him. You be good with the farm, and mind your own business, and we'll get along fine, you hear?" Travis nodded, and Bob stopped short,

"I didn't hear nothing, son." Travis looked at Bob, who was almost at eye level, and said, "I hear." Bob stared at him, "I hear, what?" Travis got it, "I hear, sir."

Bob nodded, "That's better," and turned to walk back toward the house. He was shaking his head as he yelled back over his shoulder, "Supper's at six, don't you be late. Being punctual around here will do you a lot of good."

"It helps me at work too," he added.

Three

Travis was sitting at the dining room table at five minutes before six. The girls were helping Gladys prepare the pot roast. Bob was sitting in the living room near the fireplace. He had a Budweiser beer can in his hand. He walked into the kitchen and looked at Travis.

"Son, go get me some fatwood kindling for the fire, it's down in the basement, turn left at the bottom of the stairs." Bob pointed to a door just off the kitchen. Travis hopped up and glanced at the girls as he passed them, they had stopped what they were doing, and were staring at the kitchen floor.

Travis walked through the open door, and scurried down the steps. When he reached the bottom, he heard the door slammed behind him and bolted with a board. He stood on the basement floor, confused. He smelled oil, paint, and turpentine soaked rags. There was a small, dirty window about eight feet off the ground. It looked to be about six inches by twelve inches...a narrow light was coming through, but not enough to see around him. He closed his eyes to let them adjust to the darkness.

The pitiful light coming from the window was just enough for him to see a Coleman kerosene lantern. As he walked toward the lamp a slot slid open in the door to the kitchen at the top of the stairs. "That's for not saying "Sir," the first time. Don't make the same mistake again, boy," Bob yelled.

"No, no sir" Travis yelled back, and resigned himself to sit on the cellar floor and wait. In about an hour, Travis heard a ruckus coming from upstairs. What was going on, he wondered? He walked over to the stairs and walked up three of the wooden steps, just in time to catch Tammy, as she was stumbling down the steps. Travis broke her fall, and together they landed back at the base of the stairs in a heap of bruises and splinters.

"What's going on?" Travis asked the young blonde. Tammy had been crying. Tears were running down her face and there was a large, red welt on her left cheek. "Did you forget to say sir, like I did?" She sobbed, "No, you'll find out soon enough. That's what this place, and these people are like," she whimpered.

"Bob says having time alone with me and my sister at night is the price we have to pay for living here. Tonight is Cindi's turn. Tomorrow will be mine. I feel dirty. We always feel dirty, because of him."

Travis knew what that meant, even at his age. "How long you been living here?" he asked. Tammy answered, "Three years, and we turn sixteen next month. He started in on us after the first home visit from the orphanage. They only take written reports now, because of our age, and they get copies of our report cards. Of course we're home-schooled. You will be too."

"So you've got no one to talk to, no one to tell?," Travis whispered. "No, said Tammy, Bob's even an ordained minister, he tells the state that we attend church." Tammy's tears ran and she asked, "Do you have anyone who could help?" Travis thought, "Just Lester, but he'd have to find us."

"What happened to the boy who ran away," he asked.

"Ran away? Is that what he told you? Disappeared is more like it. Bob saw Johnny, that was his name, holding hands with me, and the next day Johnny was gone. We really don't

know what happened. We hope he got away. Maybe he'll send help, but that was three months ago, so he probably didn't.""Did he ever mess with Johnny?" Travis asked, wide eyed. "No, not in that way, no," she said. "Bob just always humiliated him in front of us, trying to make himself look bigger in our eyes. "

"Johnny was meek, and small for his age, not stocky like you. But, if you're smart, you'll be meek too, avoid the beatings, that's what Gladys does. She pretends it isn't happening at all. Bob mostly lets he be, unless he's drunk. When he's drunk, he'll hit anyone." Travis was hoping he'd try. "Pick on someone your own size," he thought.

Tammy said, "Lets get the lantern, I know where the matches are." She looked at Travis in the fading light. She saw a plan forming in his mind, but didn't ask, didn't want to know.

The next morning, Gladys came down the stairs with a tray. There were two plates of food, and two iced teas. She gave each of them a list written on a small piece of yellow lined paper. "These are the chores for today. I know it's a lot of work, just be finished by the time Bob gets home at six or so." She looked at Tammy, "Cindi's not well today, you'll have to take up the slack. I've got to finish my needlepoint for Bob."

Travis' plan started to materialize in his mind. After Gladys left, he gobbled his food, looked at Tammy, and said "When I finish, I'll come in and help you out. It's under control. And don't worry. When I do a job, I want it to be done the best anyone's ever don't it. You won't have to worry about getting criticized for substandard work. "

Sure as his word, Travis worked harder than he ever had before, and more precisely too. Weeding, re-nailing downed fence, feeding the pigs and chickens, shoveling hay into the loft. All of it done perfectly, so that Bob Monroe couldn't find fault with his work. If he did his chores and had time left over to help Tammy, so what?

At 2:45 he was done. He went into the house, asked Gladys for, and received a glass of iced tea, and a refill. He asked Tammy which of the things on her list he could do for her. He took the toughest three. First he lugged the rugs and runners from the living room, hall, and dining room, out to the clothesline. He beat the dust out of them with a frenzy, took them back and replaced them exactly where they belonged.

Then he scrubbed the two large, cast iron skillets with steel wool, while wearing a pair of old work gloves he'd found in the barn. Lastly, he polished the dining room table to a high sheen which resembled a mirror when he was finished. At 5:00, they were done.

When Bob drove up at 5:45, Travis, Gladys, and the two girls were sitting on the front porch, drinking more iced tea.

Bob got out of his truck with a fierce look. He took about awhile searching around the property, inspecting the work which Travis had done that day, looking for faults. He could find none. He was pissed.

He stormed into the house, past those sitting on the porch, without a word or a glance in their direction. He smelled the country ham in the oven, and saw the place settings on the table, ready for supper. Everything was perfect.

Back out on the porch, Bob extended his hand toward Gladys, and said, "The lists, give them to me." She placed the two lists in his hand. Each item had a neat check mark beside it, noting it's completion. He looked at the list and asked Tammy, "How'd you get all this done, without Cindi's help? Tell me right now."

Tammy looked away, not wanting to be interrogated. Finally, Gladys, said to Bob, "The boy helped her, after finishing his chores. Cindi just came downstairs about an hour ago, she's feeling better."

Bob snarled at Travis, "Doin' a woman's work make you feel like a man?" Without waiting for an answer, he slapped Travis on the cheek. Travis flared red, started to respond, but held back. "Do that again, and I'll start treating you like a woman, and you won't like that, son. Not around here, you won't." Bob pointed inside, "Down to the basement, little girl. And you'll stay there just as long as I want you to."

Travis rose, looking at the floor, and walked inside, down to the basement floor. Inside his thoughts were 'my plan is working, so far.' Travis heard the door shut and bolted before he hit the last step.

After about five minutes, he started what would become a nightly ritual, push-ups and sit-ups, as many as possible. He did them until he was exhausted. He was talking to Lester all the time, going over and over his plan. It had to work the first time. Everything had to be calculated. They were, still minors. Another hundred pushups later, he collapsed, soaked with sweat.

Travis waited to see which of the girls would come tumbling down the stairs tonight, as his heart slowed from the exertion he had just put forth.

An hour later, he found out. It was Cindi, as her sister had predicted the previous evening. They sat and talked for awhile. "Tammy said she'd never have finished her chores without your help. I want you to know, we both appreciate it. It feels good to have someone on your side. Johnny was always sympathetic, but he was too afraid of Bob to stick his neck out for us."

This daily list of work chores, and evenings of nightmares, continued for the next few months. Occasionally, Bob would keep both girls with him all night, but almost all the time, Travis had company with one of the girls to talk to. He and the twins were becoming closer knit, like a real family. Travis was working on something. Both the girls knew that. They just didn't know what.

One night, both the girls were sent to the basement with Travis. Screams, curses and torments were coming from the upstairs.

Obviously, Bob had at least one too many beers. They could hear him commence to beat Gladys with his belt. The three young people heard furniture overturned, chairs slid across the linoleum kitchen floor...utter chaos.

With the three of them together, Travis saw this as an opportunity to plot. He had no idea how long it might be before the three of them had time together again.

So, he decided, tonight was the night to share his plan with his friends. He had to take the girls into his confidence, sooner or later. He would need their help to pull it off, anyway.

Travis had put on fifteen pounds of muscle through his farm chores and nightly workouts. The girls had mentioned it to him, but Bob hadn't noticed. Yes, Travis could take care of himself with Bob Monroe. He could knock him out with a frying pan, and leave.

He knew where Bob's .22 rifle was hidden, and he had found out where he kept the extra cash in the house. But, that would still leave Cindi and Tammy to absorb Bob's wrath, and take the beatings, among other things. So, in character, Travis had stayed meek, and non-confrontational with Bob.

When he helped the girls with their chores, no one said anything about it, not even Gladys. She was happy that the farm was turning a nice profit with the extra food she could sell on the side. Most of it she gave to Bob, a small amount, she squirreled away for herself.

Tonight, Travis took the girls aside, to a corner of the earthy basement. When things got a little quieter, he whispered one question. "Lester and I've got a plan. Do you want us to help you get out of this place?"

It was the first time he'd seen them smile.

"Where's Lester?" Cindi asked, looking around. Travis pointed to his chest. "In here, with me."

Four

Life was good in San Antonio for Toni (Antonia) Ramos. Last week she had received her promotion in the SAPD, to homicide lieutenant. This was her first reward for tracking down the city's first known serial killer, "The Taker," fourteen months ago. The case had been widely publicized, and was instrumental in uncovering a sophisticated money laundering operation run by several local companies. Turning drug money into "legitimate" business profits.

Toni knew the opportunity would come. Chief Perez had run for mayor, barely losing, but was guaranteed to become a city councilman, or even vice-mayor, when the new administration took over next month. He would get a treasured position which could be a stepping stone to his future political aspirations.

The chief's position had been taken by Captain Bernardo, a real working cop, and someone Toni had a great deal of respect for. Lieutenant Don Daniels moved up to Captain, with Toni taking his position, the first Latina Lieutenant.

Bernardo, Daniels, and Toni had lobbied hard, to get the job of detective, and head of the homicide squad, for 46-year old Tom Granger. He had paid his dues, and to Tom's surprise, he was promoted to the position he had always wanted, and would be very good at. Tom had discarded his "Dirty Harry" mentality, and everyone saw that as a good change. There was still the look of a 50'ish Clint Eastwood about him, but there was nothing wrong with that.

Tom had been seeing Rosa Padilla, a member of the squad, for over a year now, but they maintained a strictly professional attitude in the HQ, as well as in the field. She had lost her husband in the middle east, killed in combat. Tom lost his wife to a drunk driver, an illegal. That had been hard for him to take, but Rosa and her two girls had helped smooth his rough edges.

Toni was proud of the team she had helped build, and the new people who had been transferred into homicide had a strong foundation to learn from.

The course taken, of promoting from within the department, guaranteed a very consistent, seamless, transition in the SAPD headquarters, where each cop promoted, was already well versed in the requirements of their new assignment.

Tom Granger had the nucleus of a great team of investigators. First was Billy Cheatham, the ex-rodeo bull rider. He was a nicely packaged 6'3", who now specialized in another kind of bull. He had never really "grown up," but was a great cop.

Then, Starr Jones, mid-twenties, smart, black, attractive, and getting better every day. Rosa Padilla, an experienced investigator who was the best interrogator in the entire squad. Rosa was the consummate officer in actions and appearance, although she was a bit on the stocky side.

Now the real pressure was placed directly on Toni's shoulders. Two murders just last week-end. Fortunately, and sadly, they were basically common crimes. In one, a poker game turned accusation and disrespect into a macho drunken gunfight, one dead, one injured. Being disrespected, or the perception of such an act, was the Main cause of wrongful death in San Antonio.

The second killing, was a domestic dispute where a wife had stabbed her abusive husband to death while he was sleeping. Cut and dried. She didn't dispute the fact that she had killed him, bemoaning she hadn't done it sooner.

Toni had heard that the murdering wife had been to the emergency room four times in the past eighteen months for "falling down stairs," or tripping over a rug, so maybe the D.A. would cut her some slack. However that wasn't Toni's decision. She was glad of that.

It was getting close to the Holiday Season. Obviously, someone forgot to inform the local gangs. There had been three "drive by" shootings in the past couple of weeks. Fortunately there were only people wounded, no deaths. Being "gang-related" kept it out of Toni's already crowded schedule, as these incidents were being handled by the gang squad.

This time of the year was great for kids, families, relatives, and spouses...something Toni had none of. But, the squad always celebrated together...as a family. That's the way cops usually feel about their co-workers, year round. The Holidays just seemed to bring them all a little closer. And she had her best friend, Rhonda.

Tonight was girls night with Rhonda, her closest and most long-time friend. Theirs was not a stressful relationship. Toni and Rhonda Fleming, had been friends since high school and roommates their last two years at UTSA. Rhonda was a person Toni was comfortable with. They didn't have to impress each other.

The thirty one year old Toni, had jet-black hair she wore cut business length short. She dressed professionally. Her light brown Hispanic complexion needed no help from makeup. She had kept her 5'9" frame in shape, thanks to will power and her gym. Toni couldn't run marathons any longer after an ACL injury, but she was determined to keep the weight off.

Rhonda was exactly the opposite, except for the fitness. She was very petite, 5' 2," topping out at 105 pounds, and was a fiery redhead, part of her signature. She always dressed in the latest style, when in public...it was her business. They had other things in common which also made them close, Toni thought.

Neither one of them had big families. Toni was an only child, with both her parents deceased from cancer while she was in school. Rhonda had a sister in St. Louis, who was living the "soccer mom" life which left her no time to remain close.

Then, it was the men, or better said, the scarcity of men in their lives. They hadn't gone out of their way to discourage traditional relationships. Their chosen career paths were enough to do that.

For Toni, being a police officer was an anti-involvement shield. Her work intimidated some men, yes. It was also the 80-hour week with unpredictable hours.

Emergency cell phone calls had ruined more than one relationship for Toni. Go to a restaurant for a nice dinner, begin to have a pleasant conversation, only to be summoned to a crime scene in the middle of the entree. "The Job," was difficult to compete with, Toni admitted to herself.

Rhonda was kept busy, at about the same pace as Toni. She had three small retail boutiques. One was on the River Walk, the second store was at North Star Mall, the city's largest shopping center with Macy's, Saks, and a pair of 40-ft tall cowboy boots in the parking lot.

She had opened her third store in Austin, about an hour and a half drive up I-35, in Highland Mall, about a year ago and had been a huge success. There were lots of petite shoppers in a college town.

Her newest store was a one-of-a-kind, just as her others were. She wasn't looking to franchise the business model, and wanted to stay ahead of the pack. She specialized in smaller sizes of designer clothing for juniors and women.

She had a few shoes and bags on the side, but her shops, appropriately named "The Collection" did 90% of their business in fashion forward dresses and smart casual attire, over half of her sales in sizes 0-6. This was a small portion of the demographic, but these ladies had a tough time finding the right clothes without going to New York or Los Angeles. Rhonda was becoming a big hit in the retail fashion world.

Tonight, however, would be jeans, sandals, a t-shirt, and stir-fried Chinese. They got together at least twice a month. Tonight was Toni's turn, and she had selected the menu. Rhonda came over at 7, with two bottles of pinot grigio, and the women decided to have a glass, and decompress, on the small lanai off Toni's small backyard.

As always, the very best part of their friendship was that they never, ever, talked about their business, or their personal lives. Books, movies, star gossip, and the state of the world, were enough. They had made a habit of swapping books at every informal dinner, and tonight they had brought each other the same book, "The Girl With The Dragon Tattoo" by Stieg Larssen. They both laughed till they cried.

Such was friendship.

Five

It was after work on a beautiful Friday. Bob Monroe had just finished a big painting job on a new state building. He received his last "draw" today for the work. The state held back their usual 5% in escrow, insuring that the punch list items and touch-up work would be done within the next 45 days. Bob always worried about the escrow. But what the hell, he bid the job for "Behr, cottage white", and substituted an inexpensive brand, making several hundred extra dollars to begin with. He knew they'd never recognize the difference.

Now it was on to the weekend, a few beers to sleep on, and the king would rule his castle for two days. Bob was just thinking how he had made himself a great life. Yeah, it took cutting corners, and some lying, plus that thing with the girls, but he was living it up, enjoying life. He had handled the obstacles, like that boy Johnny. Nobody would ever find where he'd hid his body.

Bob drove up the driveway, Gladys, and the girls were sitting on the porch, as usual. Bob got out of his paint truck and demanded, "Where's the boy?"

Gladys looked down at the floor. She knew Bob was most abusive on weekends, he would be off the next day, and could drink as much as he wanted. "He took sick, late this afternoon. Something in his belly. He was rolling around, moaning and wailing, something awful. You know, it could be his appendix, I was gonna call Dr. Whiteside, see if he would look at him, but I wanted to wait till you got home."

Bob snorted, "We don't need no doctors, or any other strangers around here. You're lucky you didn't call him."

At the same time, angry, Bob knew that he needed Travis. Between running the farm and the monthly state foster parent checks, he had stashed away several thousand dollars. He needed Travis, alright. And he needed him healthy. He might have to risk a trip to the emergency room.

Bob said, "I'll go take a look at him. Where is he, down in the basement?" Gladys nodded and she followed Bob inside, then stopping and sitting at the dining room table. They were almost immediately met with another howl from Travis, "My stomach hurts, help me," he screamed. Bob scurried down the stairs, sniffing the air full of flammables. This wasn't right, boom! When he stepped on the fifth step, about 4 feet from the bottom, it was like he had stepped into a swimming pool. The tred broke, right in the middle. His right leg went through the board, the stairs coming up to his to his knee.

Bob stumbled forward, and tried to recover, but the next step he made, with his left foot, cracked that board in the very same place. Bob fell forward from the waist up, helpless. He saw Travis reach for him, grabbing his painting coveralls on both sides of his neck. The boy pulled Bob downward as hard as he could, and Bob heard the snap of his right lower leg bones, breaking like twigs. He slumped forward, trapped with his head below his feet, arms flailing about, screaming in pain for someone to help him.

Bob turned towards the top of the stairs as much as possible, begging anyone for help. He saw his wife,

Gladys, perfectly outlined in the doorway above. She had heard the commotion and was trying to figure out what had happened. Gladys now saw Bob's predicament. Then she saw a big smile appear on Travis' face. What was that about, she thought.

The two girls were directly behind Gladys, and together, they shoved her down the stairs toward the basement floor. Gladys cart wheeled and landed like a sack of flour on the steps, splitting her head open as she continued her fall to the floor. Bob looked at Travis and just before he passed out from the pain, he knew he wouldn't be collecting that escrow check from the state.

Gladys lay there bleeding, a fairly large scalp wound produced lots of blood. But she was breathing. Out cold, but alive. Travis knew that the "alive" status was only a temporary situation.

Six

The plan was perfect, so far. That afternoon Travis had cut through about 80% of the bottom five steps of the stairs. He had used an old hack saw he had found in the barn.

The cellar, already a fire trap, was made even more so by him and Cindi the previous night. They had spread the oily rags and turpentine throughout the cellar floor. Now they just needed a spark.

Travis reached behind a support beam, and grabbed the full Coleman lantern and matches. He scurried up past an unconscious Bob, on the outside of the 2 x 6s the stairs were nailed to. Once he got past the sixth step, he walked to the top and inside the kitchen / cellar door. He turned and smiled at the girls.

He let Tammy light the lantern, and he tossed it to the basement floor, where it shattered, followed by a sudden "whoosh" of ignition. They closed the door, but didn't bolt it. There was no way either of the Monroes would make it up the stairs. The three teenagers could already feel the heat from the cellar.

Travis looked at the girls, "You packed?" they both nodded and he scampered up to their bedroom, retrieving battered old cardboard suitcases the girls had hidden under their bed. He detoured to the attic entrance, pulled down the folded steps, and grabbed the box he knew held the Monroes' cash reserves. After only thirty seconds in the attic, Travis ran down the stairs yelling, "The living room," timing was essential. They only had a few minutes until this place would become fatal for anyone who was inside.

The three conspirators rushed to the living room. Travis gave the girls an envelope with over fourteen thousand dollars in cash. The Monroe's life savings. The Monroes wouldn't be needing it. He kept $200 for himself.

There was a Greyhound bus station less than two miles away. The girls could get to it on back roads before it got too dark. All they had to do was pick a place of destination, and go. They were almost seventeen now, and could pass for being older.

They had an aunt in Charleston who Bob had let them stay in touch with. He screened the letters, but allowed them to write her. They had said that they might go there. "I don't want to know," Travis had said, "just get out of here."

Travis kissed them both on the forehead and said, "Go, while you still have some light." Cindi appealed, "Please go with us, please." Travis was tempted, but he declined.

"Every time you girls would look at me, you'd think of this place, and what happened to you here. You need to forget all this, and get a fresh start with your lives. Besides, I need to stay here and see this through. To do the job right."

Travis knew that an abandoned house with two dead

adults, would bring questions. He wanted to be here to sell his story. "I'll tell the police you left months ago. Now get on the road." The girls left, and Travis walked outside in the yard, and stood 50 feet from the house, watching their backs get smaller in the distance. They were scared, but happy. They'd eventually be fine.

Travis Bayne, would not be fine, ever again.

After about five minutes the house was engulfed in flame. Black smoke was pouring out the doors and windows. Nothing could survive that. Travis ran the quarter mile to the main road and flagged down the first vehicle he saw, a red Chevy pickup. "My house is burning, please help us."

The driver said, "Son, get in." Travis shook his head wildly, and yelled, "Tell the fire department it's the Monroe place. I've got to go back and see if I can help," and he ran back toward the house.

Thirty minutes later, two fire engines pulled up in front of a rapidly burning house. Travis had rubbed his clothes with some soot, so it looked like he had attempted a rescue. He was sitting at the end of the driveway with his head in his hands. He had thought about the girls' ordeal, which helped bring tears to his eyes.

The fire brigade started dousing the flames with water, but there was nothing left they could do. After an hour or so, it was safe to go into the house. Later, a fireman came out shaking his head. Travis overheard him tell the fire marshal in charge, "Two people, fried. Hard to tell, but it could be a man and a woman." The fire chief replied, "Well, that goes with what the boy, here said. He was in the field, the man came home drunk."

"It's a Friday. Probably a tradition for him. One that got him killed."

"Yeah," said the first firefighter, "and there's plenty of these, all empty, scattered in the basement," showing one of the charred Budweiser beer cans Travis had planted down there in the past few days.

"Yeah, look at the truck over there. He was a painter," said the chief. "Probably was drunk and careless, stored his supplies downstairs so he could get to them no matter what the weather. That's why the fire didn't take long to burn out."

Over the next few days, Travis told his story, always the exact same story, to the police, fire marshal, sheriff, social services, and to the South Raleigh High School.

Only the three of them lived in the house, the Stone twins had run away months ago. He had been home-schooled, and well-treated, but the girls had a rough time. He wanted to plant that seed, so it might not happen as easily in the future. More supervision was needed.

The state sent him to the high school for evaluation. He had been home-schooled (supposedly), and they wanted to know his capabilities. The school administered the SAT and some other intelligence tests, and Travis scored well. He was almost eighteen, so the powers that were at Social Services decided he could live and work part-time at the orphanage. He had a reputation as a hard worker among those he knew there. In his previous stints at the facility he had created a positive image of himself. Of course they didn't know what he had been through with the Monroes. How could they have imagined?

The school said that he could even try out for the football or baseball teams, if he kept his grades up. They thought he had done very well for himself, especially with the hand he had been dealt. For one boy to go through three sets of foster parents, with each placement ending so tragically, was enough to break lesser souls. Or, enough to temper steel, which it had done with Travis.

This episode, this portion of Travis' young life had cemented his *Inclination.*

His die had been cast. His smiling, boyish, demeanor hid his latent instincts...sometimes. But, Lester was still there, inside.

His senior year in high school started in just a couple of months. He put a great deal of time in the summer in the library, as well as with his daily workouts. He was also able to begin to develop some speed, and he had God-given agility. He wanted to play football, and as it turned out, he was good at it.

After he graduated, high school, he played a decent middle linebacker in the JUCO (junior college) league for two years, on a football scholarship. Travis Bayne even made "all-conference," his second year in college.

He was a violent player, who liked to punish people who came into his territory. He loved playing football, and dishing out the hits.

When his coach came over and whispered to Travis "put number 32 out of the game," that's what he did, clean or dirty, same result, no problem.

He had talents, Travis was very fast, with a body and a temperament perfect for football. Even though he had an IQ measured at 170, he never really applied himself to schoolwork after high school. He saw no benefit to it.

As it turned out, his mediocre junior college grades and more importantly, his psychological tests, kept him out of the 4-year schools. As you might expect, he could be an intimidating person to interview. One moment he would be evasive and shy, the next belligerent. His football, and his schooling, were at the end of the road.

Seven

He joined the Army at 20, he did two tours in Iraq. This is where he was selected and trained to be a sniper, hunter, and survivor. He was the best his instructors had seen, "a natural," his Master Sergeant had commented.

After his second tour, certain, civilian, people had plans for Travis. During his time in Iraq, he was known to the enemy by two names, "The Wind of Death," or "The Night Butcher." The distinction was derived from whether the "kill" was long range or close up. The victims from a close kill were almost always missing an ear. It was his signature One hot summer day the Army finally discharged Travis. He was told that he had served his country proudly.

At discharge, he had his first meeting with the "suits." Men wearing coats and ties in 100+ degree weather, inside a Quonset hut with the windows blacked out. The only thing normal about them was that they were wearing sun glasses. Travis was told that he could be an even greater service to his country, at a better, tax-free, pay scale. He didn't hesitate. It was all he knew.

He simply went where the men in suits and ties sent him. "Black Ops" in South or Central America, or just as likely some small African nation who was our enemy one day, and our friend the next. Qatar, Chad, Manila, Damascus, he was always on the move. He pulled "shadow duty" for 4 years. The elimination of terrorists and traitors was easy for him. Wet-work, was his specialty.

Wherever he was ordered to go, he had but one intent, one singular mission. He was proud that he had always completed his assignment. This was job #1. He always took his target "out of the game."

His escape or his own quick death, was obviously job #2. But it was only an expedient preference for his employers. They didn't have a replacement ready, but there was a long list of candidates. As Hank Williams Sr. sang, "I'll never get out of this world alive." Didn't Hank just know it? But it didn't bother Travis. He had cheated the grim reaper, time and again, and he'd already met the Devil.

The elimination of terrorists and traitors was easy for him. The end justified the means, he had read somewhere. The Army had helped build a perfect killer. Not just some dumb ass who fired Howitzer shells from miles away.

Travis could do it from over one thousand yards with his Browning 50 M1022 sniper rifle, he kept broken down in his back pack, even today. Ah, yes the Browning.

The Browning had been made famous by USMC Gunnery Sgt. Carlos Hathcock in 1967. He had 93 confirmed kills in Viet Nam, probably twice that, which he and his spotter hadn't stayed around to verify.

Hathcock had died of M.S. in 1999, in Virginia Beach, Virginia. Travis read a small article in the Norfolk paper when he traveled through that year.

Eight lines...just eight lines on a single column, as an obituary for a decorated war hero. Hathcock had sat on a hilltop overlooking a densely, overgrown plain for ten days. On one side of the plain was a platoon of 24 Marines, some badly wounded, but the area was deemed "too hot" (or too far into Cambodia) for a helicopter evac. the opposite side of this killing field were estimated to be 600 North Vietnamese regulars. The enemy kept trying to overrun the heavily outnumbered Marines. This would have been a great achievement for them.

It would be even more celebrated than when they had massacred the French, during their own debacle in that small Asian country. Carlos would not let that happen. Not on his watch. Carlos kept killing the enemy as they tried to cross the plain. Some tried speed, others stealth, none got through. And none were ever included in the 93 confirmed kills.

Hathcock had gotten by on 3-4 hours sleep, usually in the heat of the day, and only when his spotter was awake. He had nothing to eat for the last 6 days he was there. A small spring, ten yards away, gave them water. That's why he had chosen this site. On the eleventh day, Marine reinforcements had marched in behind a curtain of napalm. Hathcock and his spotter vanished into the jungle. They both showed up at a Marine camp, 90 days later, looking like nothing had ever happened.

Eight lines.

While in Vietnam, Carlos Hathcock's longest confirmed kill had been 2,500 yards, a quick conversion told Travis that was over 1.4 miles. The record had stood for a very long time, exceeded only in Afghanistan in 2002, by a team of Canadians, no less, 35 years later. Travis wasn't in that league, but he was still excellent. And he was going to get more than eight lines.

As good as he was with a rifle, Bayne was even better than the at killing up close.

He woke at night, seeing the last look of horror on an enemies' face, the death rattle of a punctured lung grasping for oxygen, the smell of fear, when the outcome was realized by his victim. But kept killing, those had always been his orders. Being a sniper, or a night stalker, no difference to Travis. He was good at it.

But, then, deep into his second tour, came the assignment which marked him for life. It was a horrible mistake, and one that could have been easily avoidable. The intel team back at Baghdad had targeted a 30 x 50 foot, single story mud building for eradication. Nothing new here.

Travis had staked out this particular target out for 5 days, from several angles. He was even bold enough to briefly infiltrate the building. It was easy, no guards, like you would you would expect to find, in fact, no men at all. Something wasn't right. And he wanted to get to the bottom of it. The mission was a mistake...had to be, and he wanted the intelligence officers to know it.

That night, Travis slowly crawled back about 500 yards, to a spot inside an outcropping of rocks. This was his "fall-back" position in case he had to make an unexpected exit.

He had dug a 3 x 5 foot hole about 3 feet deep in the mixture of rocks and sandy soil. It had taken him he better part of 2 nights to accomplish this. Inside, and protectively wrapped against sand and the elements, was buried his emergency equipment stash for a hasty retreat.

It included a collection of RPG's, two mortars, the deadliest rifle built, which was a Barrett 50 caliber, and an encrypted satellite phone. The phone was untraceable, but he still tried to make the conversations only during what he deemed an emergency.

After only a minute or two his handler, code named "Zebra," was on the line. Travis had de-briefed him in person, once, along with his superior. He knew "Zebra's" real name was Ron McShay. His boss had gone by the name of Reynolds.

Travis was certain that a mistake had been made in targeting this particular site. He asked "Zebra" to stand down, at least for 24 hours, He would perform a full visual recon on the inside of the store. His Kurdish was better than most, and you would be amazed at what a little pointing and grunting could accomplish.

After all, the natives spoke dialects of Arabic, Persian, and Aramaic. The building was a bakery storefront, but was actually acting as a "birthing center" which provided assistance for difficult deliveries, breech births and the like. It was also a violation of Sharia law.

One of our Iraqi "allies" had planted information which would provide two victories. The destruction of the women's center would be used as propaganda by the extremist... "against the will of Allah" etc., and secondly, it would be blamed on the Americans.

This "ally" was obviously an agent planted in the center of our intelligence operation. He knew that he would be rewarded very well, monetarily. And, if discovered later and eventually martyred, he held the vision of 72 virgins awaiting him in paradise, close to his heart.

Despite Travis' protestations, begging for more time to observe, the intelligence community had made up their minds. McShay, and Reynolds gave the mission the green light.

The CIA had believed their own, well paid, informants over his word. Or they owed a debt which must be paid for with innocent lives. On that cold winter night in January, the CIA advised one of their U.S.A.F. flight teams, thousands of miles away in Creech AFB, Indian Springs, Nevada, to launch. The "flyer" with the joystick control, sent the drone on it's way.

The weapon was a "MQ-1A, Predator", a drone aircraft equipped with 2-AGM "Hellfire" missiles. The pilotless plane rocketed down a short runway from some remote airstrip in the Middle East. Flying time was eighteen minutes. The longest eighteen minutes of his young life, so far.

Travis had been advised to pull back from the target area at least one quarter mile. He was well outside of that range, but the detonation shook the ground as if they had been nuked.

The two Hellfire missiles struck the target simultaneously. The resulting damage left nothing larger than a woman's fist, from what had been a shelter of mercy. There were many more bodies on the ground, than loaves of bread.

Of course, the Americans said it was a top level insurgent meeting, involving several of al-Qaeda's upper echelon.

The Iraqi's, more or less kept quiet. All of the local men claimed to have no knowledge of anything beyond that of the business being a bakery, creating Meza, Kabhz, Saloom, and the pastries, including Burek. The women who had organized the shelter, knew that their death by stoning would not bring their slaughtered sisters back. They would find another place for their merciful acts. Travis thought that they were the real heroes in this war.

This act of brutality against innocent civilians was the final straw. It was the only time he had been involved in a "cover-up." He could file a report which would never see the light of day, but what would that accomplish?

No, Travis knew the men he had previously killed under orders, had much blood on their hands. They were gun runners, genocidal mass murderers, and traffickers in human slavery. They received what they deserve, whether they worshiped God, Allah, or Buddha. Each of them already had reservations for hell. Travis just provided the transportation.

He made a life-changing decision that day. He would eventually have his own mission. His final tour of duty. It would be called "Payback." First he had to flush his targets out into the open. Then they were to pay for their sins...but not with money.

He kept up his covert operations for the "suits" for another year. He spent as much time as possible getting the necessary things he would need to disappear and live "off the grid". In his line of work, he had plenty of connections. He managed to acquire three passports, four U.S. driver's licenses from various states, a Social Security card from a dead childbirth, and other ID's he would need in order to vanish.

One Thursday, the "Company" knew where he was. Three days later at check in time, he didn't use the Sat phone with his code name, which ominously, was "Reaper."

His handlers speculated that maybe Travis was in a compromised position, and couldn't call in. So, they waited 2 more days until they reached out for him. An effort which produced zero.

A man like Travis, with five days head start, could be in Montana or Mongolia by now. A system-wide alert was issued. The SAS, FBI, CIA, Mossad, and others were on the watch for a man they described as a "traitor."

Travis had now started his final mission. A tour with only one possible outcome, for him.

Those who were initially sent out to find and terminate him, met a quick death. No torturing, no slow ending to their lives. They were just following orders like he had once done. Travis would be 32 years old this Spring.

After avoiding detection for three years, out of the system, he felt a somewhat safer. Never safe, but safer.

The screams from the "bakery" that fateful night haunted him every day.

McShay and Reynolds had never left his mind. They had both been promoted...to the U.S. How accommodating. He knew where McShay lived, but not Reynolds, so he would have to "do them" together. If one heard of the other's death, he could put 2+2 together. And, he was starting to get the attention of the those he wanted revenge upon. Travis knew them well. If he made enough noise, eventually McShay and Reynolds would have to come for him themselves. He looked forward to that tour of duty. It didn't take much, maybe just the appearance of his acts or his trademark, caused paranoia among the ones who recognized the significance of a missing ear.

Travis wondered if they knew that he was coming for them. It wouldn't make a difference in the outcome, just a little enjoyment in knowing that they feared him.

Book Two

Eight

Travis returned to the present. It was a fresh, new day. For almost three years he had kept moving, always in the U.S., and then, mostly in the south. It was much easier to travel here.

Most of his trip was through small, podunk towns, and even there, no, especially there, people could sense that he was trouble, hopefully, just passin' through. Travis was walking west on Highway 90. He had just crossed the Mississippi state line. The sign read: "Pascagoula...28m." Travis had seen that sign on this road, at least two or three times before.

It had been two days since he had eaten anything other than "road kill," and Thanksgiving was just last week. He saw it advertised on a shoe store sign. It was Christmas coming up in the next few weeks. It would get colder here at night, but almost never freeze.

Travis hated the cold, and timed his trips to avoid the full brunt of a nasty winter. This part of the country was refreshing to Travis. A much slower pace, some salt in the air from the nearby Gulf of Mexico, and trees... mostly tall pines.

He'd need to find some work here to get some money for the next leg of his trip. Any job, it could be shoveling oyster shells, clearing land, tending to animals, anything for a couple of weeks. He was somewhat skilled at repairs and improvising. The Army taught you that. He'd get enough money to travel with.

Then he'd continue on his mission. He typically traveled the deep south in the winter, then turned slightly north as spring began and east as the weather warmed.

The smaller, rural places like rural areas were perfect for him to accomplish his work. He knew his prey would come after him. It was part of his walking tour of America. A tour where he played "catch me if you can." They hadn't yet.

He especially enjoyed the small towns, with adjacent jurisdictions. And this part of his itinerary was his favorite. It was only 170 miles from Florida to Louisiana...four states, lots of tiny towns and jurisdictions on the now, little-used Highway 90.

Most drivers were in a rush to get from point "A" to point "B." So, the most traffic would travel the parallel interstate, I-10. Travis was in no hurry. Travis was on his journey, looking for work to get by. Walk awhile, then catch a ride, mostly in the back of a pick-up truck. Didn't much matter to Travis, as long as they were headed in his direction. Sometimes he was able to get some information from the diver.

In these small towns, everyone knew everyone else. Who needed temporary help. A farm had a crop to bring in, the death of a husband who owned 50 cows, or had corn to turn under, a barn repair, whatever. These types of jobs weren't posted in the paper.

Travis got lucky, later that day. A local trucker, hauling

heating oil stopped to pick him up. He was still on Highway 90, in Mississippi, just east of Pascagoula, when the big truck's air brakes came to a squealing stop.

The driver was a heavy set man, wearing black-rimmed glasses with shades clipped over them. He had a tuft of salt & pepper hair on the sides, but not much. He looked to be about 5'8," 285 pounds. Travis figured the driver would die of a heart attack in the next 5 years. Empty sacks and wrappers from Burger King and Taco Bell, littered the floorboard. The scent of French fries hung in the stale air. This was like world cholesterol headquarters.

As Travis got in, he thanked and introduced himself to the man as "Tim Turner, thanks for the lift." The trucker, gave his name back as Earl. "Just look at the sign on the truck." "Earl the Oil Man," it said. He extended his beefy hand and apologized. "Glad to give you a ride, excuse the mess, and the cigarette smell."

"Ain't supposed to smoke while I'm doin' this, but it's my own business, right? I make my own rules, and really don't have time for much lunch, much less the clean up. The whole county wants their oil yesterday, like it's going to snow down here or something." He laughed about that, "You know it did snow ten or twelve years ago, and the temperature rose to 58 degrees that same day. I usually only fill the tanks 90% anyway, The other 10% is my retirement money."

Travis smiled back. He could tell the man had plenty of lunch, lately. Cigarettes, too. The truck's ashtray was overflowing.

Earl was making conversation, Travis was careful what he answered. The driver asked, looking at the backpack, "ex-military, are you, Tim?"

"No," Travis lied, "got out of the Merchant Marines a few years back. My brother has a car business up in Meridian. Said he could use the help. I'm good with engines. You have to learn a lot about how things work, when your ship breaks down halfway to the Panama canal, especially near Cuban waters."

Earl nodded like he knew exactly what Tim, or rather Travis, was saying.

Travis asked "Maybe you can point me in the right direction, Earl. I'm looking for a temporary job, just a month or so, nothing special, but something so I won't show up in Meridian flat broke. The sister-in-law wouldn't cotton to that, I'm sure."

"Today may be your lucky day, Tim, my man. I'm headed up to Chester and Eunice Tate's farm in Moss Point, right now. Their boy just ran off with a waitress from the I-Hop about 2 weeks ago. Haven't heard hide nor hair from him, and work is piling up at the farm."

Earl explained, "You know, Chester has a bad leg, and can't do much himself. He could use somebody like you to help square things up. He's got over 150 acres, crops are in, but there's lots to be done to get ready for the winter and spring."

The big man continued, "If he doesn't do the prep work now, his crop harvest will be half of what it usually is."

"That's my next stop, it's a few miles from here, I'll give you an intro and see if you can work something out with Chester while I'm filling their tank. They're good folks"

"That would be my lucky day," Travis said with an appreciative tone. Really all I'll need is room and board, plus some cash at the end of each week. If they have a barn, I can sleep out there, it's still in the 60's at night here. Used to love sleeping on the deck of a big freighter," he embellished.

In a very few minutes they were driving up a long oyster shell driveway. It was perfect. Travis couldn't see any other neighboring houses. The main structure was 200 yards off the road, almost enveloped in pine trees, and it was up a slight incline.

There was a barn, a detached 2-car garage, a covered area for a John Deere and a "bush hog," next to a shed, where tools were obviously stored. An older man was limping out of the shed pushing a wheelbarrow with a shovel and hoe sticking out.

Chester waved when he saw Earl's truck, as Earl continued up the long driveway. Travis had on his "Good Travis" face, with behavior to match. He could be charming, like now, smiling ear to ear. "Big Earl, where you been? This is the latest I seen you in 20 years, Chester ribbed."

"Well Chester, people been waiting for oil prices to go down, and they didn't. Now they all want it before it gets higher. And here I am, thought I's doing you a favor. Brought you a man looking for work. His name's

Tim Turner, ex of the merchant marine, and someone I highly recommend you use to get your property back in good shape. Any news from that no-count son of yours?"

"None, and at this point I ain't got no use for him either, his mother would probably take him back, though." Chester was small built, with a "hawkish" nose, and had something of a beer belly hanging down behind his overalls. "Anyway, son," he turned to Travis, "Chester Tate's the name, and you're Tim? Whatcha good at?"

Travis answered in the vernacular he had picked up from this conversation. "Hard work, carpentry, painting, plumbing, fixin' anything that needs fixin', you name it."

"One thing about bein' on a big ship for a long time, you got to learn how things work, and you got to know what to do when they break down. Ain't no handy repairman when you're a thousand miles out to sea. Got to do it yourself, and if you can't fix it the right way the first time, things get real bad." Truth was, Travis was handy with machinery, and could do a passable carpentry job.

Chester looked him up and down, sizing the man up, and then pointed at the tractor, "Drive that John Deere over yonder?" Travis answered, "Towing the bush hog, behind me...no problem."

"I'll fill up both of the oil tanks, let you two alone to talk business," Earl said. "You did want both of them full I guess," he added. Chester nodded that that was what he was expecting and Earl pulled his rig up to the two filling valves for the underground tanks.

After Earl walked away, Travis looked at Mr. Tate convincingly, "All I need is room and board, I'll sleep in the barn. My pay would be $150 a week in cash, at the end of the week. You can let me go anytime you like, no hard feelings. I heard you had a son. He comes back tomorrow, you don't need me anymore, I'm gone, no harm done.

Plus, no paperwork, no tax problems, I can stay 2 weeks or as long as 8, I'll put in 60 hours a week, except on Sundays, when I spend time alone praying. I'm sorta old fashioned about Sundays, but how does that sound?"

"You can start now, Tate asked?" "Yessir," Travis replied. "Then today is my lucky day." Chester Tate said.

It wasn't!

The two men walked around the property closest to the house and barn. Chester was pointing out areas of the farm which needed the most work, and detailing what kind of crop he had planted in the past. It was a familiarity thing for Chester. Travis viewed it as a scouting mission.

"No dog?" Travis asked. "Naw." Chester replied, "Had one ten years ago. All this wild game out here, the dog'd be yapping all night long. When he died, I never replaced him. Slept like a baby ever since." Travis just nodded, happy inside.

Chester commented, "This here's my wife, Eunice," he said nodding to a portly woman with a beehive hairdo.

Travis spent the next two weeks with carpentry work,

repairs, and general labor. He was working 10-12 hours a day, impressing Chester and Eunice.

He was out of bed and on the job by 6 a.m. everyday. Sometimes he told them he was too busy for lunch, that wasn't the real reason, but he almost always cleaned up and sat down with them at supper time. It was time spent getting to know the house, and the people.

After the meal, the two men would walk out the back door through the screen porch and discuss the list of things to be worked on the next day. This meant that Chester had gone to "Fred's Hardware and Paint," 5 miles away, and purchased the materials, whether it be paint, or lumber, whatever was needed to complete the work.

Travis was always too busy to go to the store. He didn't want them to them be seen together. Chester would pull his 1992, Ford F-150 pickup out of the detached garage and drive into Moss Point to buy whatever Travis had told him he would need when they first walked the farm and noted the work to be done. The first week he'd even bought a new pair of work gloves for his helper. Travis had mentioned that gloves would help him avoid blisters, splinters, and such. They would also obscure fingerprints.

What Travis was really doing at lunchtime was scouting, and getting to know the Tate's better. At the lunches he missed, he would sit on his bunk and listen to their conversation through a tiny "bug" he had stuck under the kitchen table. It only had a range of 500 yards, but that was plenty for his purposes. This way they could discuss things "privately." Travis heard every word on his tiny receiver.

He discovered during one of these lunches, another piece of good news. Their only daughter lived in San Francisco, and she never called, even on Holidays, not on Christmas or on their birthdays. No dog, no close neighbors or friends, no communication with their relatives...perfect.

In the beginning, they were somewhat wary. This was to be expected. But, by the second week, they both considered him a "Godsend"... a real life saver when they most needed it. The opposite was of course, true.

Eunice left the house only twice a week, at most. Every other Saturday she went to "Barbara's Hair Boutique," and then to the grocery store, for the week's meals she had planned.

Sunday, the Tates went to the Moss Point Baptist Church from 11 to 2. They had invited him to go with them, but he always declined. He kept a King James Bible on the small table beside his bunk in the barn, to maintain his Christian façade.

The barn floor was dirt, covered with a thick layer of straw, and a cast iron wood stove on a slab of bricks to be used if it really got cold, that wouldn't be needed till much later.

Travis had their routine down to the minute. One Sunday, while the couple was at church, he searched the house, looking for stashed money. Country people like this didn't trust banks. They'd been warned by their parents of bank failures, runs, panic, and the like. He'd need the money.

That day, he found out something else about the Tates. They were peddlers of child pornography. While scanning their computer, he found a shortcut named 5 & 10. He clicked on that, which opened up dozens of more shortcuts to sites, mainly of naked children from age 5 to 10. This was inhuman. He hadn't planned to hurt them, but this wasn't right.

But, Travis continued his search that Sunday. He didn't want jewelry or such. That could be traced.

He found the cash in the third place he looked. After the freezer, he checked the living room book collection to see if any had been hollowed out, and then found the loose board in the floor of the closet in the master bedroom.

Around ten thousand dollars...not much, but probably all they had. He knew they owned the farm and acreage "outright" so they didn't need much more than their social security checks to live on.

Travis put the board back in place carefully, putting the shoe boxes on the floor exactly like the mental picture he took when he opened the closet door. This would be for later.

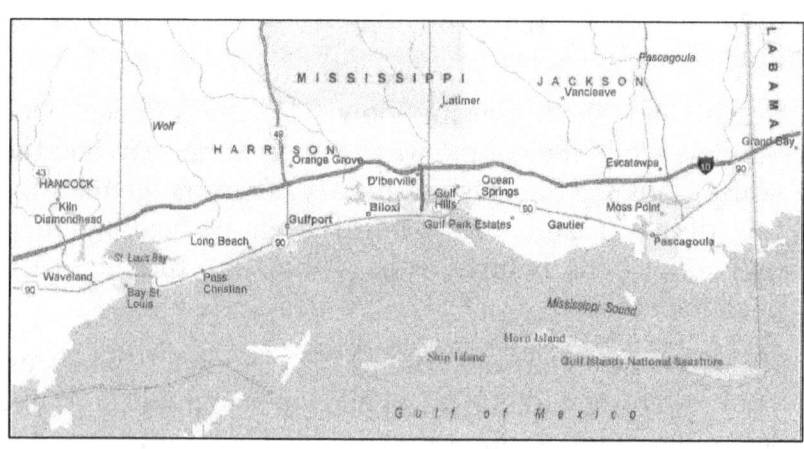

Nine

It was a peaceful Friday night in Slidell, Louisiana. The familiar hooting of an old owl perched on an oak limb covered in Spanish moss broke the silence, occasionally. He was just looking for his supper. This is what he did.

Laverne Thibodeaux woke screaming from her nightmare. Her nightgown was drenched in sweat, but she had the chills. Claude, her husband of 28 years startled out of his deep sleep and grabbed the Winchester over/under he kept beside the bed. Then he realized, the dreams were back.

"It was the man again, wasn't it?" Claude asked. "The evil one you see coming for you."

Laverne was sobbing. "I thought he was gone. I haven't had a vision of him in almost a year."

They had been to see their family doctor last December, almost a year ago. She'd had these fearsome sleeps for a couple of years, but they were getting worse. Curiously, they always happened around the Holiday season.

Dr. Dufort had given her some mild sleeping pills, they didn't help much. However, after a couple of weeks, the dreams began to subside, both in frequency and intensity.

The last one she had before tonight was January 20th of this year. She remembered the date because it was exactly one week before her birthday. An early present, she had called it. The type of gift she wanted no part of.

Now it was starting again. She couldn't explain the visions she had of something evil, maybe sent by the devil, himself, coming her way, getting closer, the dreams growing stronger.

She knew the spirit was intent on doing evil. Laverne couldn't describe it. It was in the shape of a charred man but his face, his eyes looked like they were on fire...yes, pools of fire, she called them.

It was 3 am, and Claude paced the floor of their ranch home. It was located on the eastern outskirts of town just off South Military Road. It was convenient for Claude. He raised hogs and goats on his 30 acres, and getting them to market was less than 5 miles away. It had been his daddy's land before he passed, and had been owned by the family since before the war. Around these parts, that meant the Civil War, and to Claude and many of his friends, it wasn't over yet.

He worked his farm hard, even as his arthritic joints creaked with occasional pain. Claude didn't care what a man did for a living, as long as he had a job, or at least was earnestly looking for work. The "no counts," as his grandfather had told him came in all colors. There were plenty of blacks he did business with. Hard workers who he would pitch in and help anytime and extra back or pair of hands was needed.

He just didn't sit too well with those that thought they were owed a living, just by being born. He didn't like the ones who had a feeling of entitlement, no matter what their race. Hell, rats could breed, nothing special about that. A man ought to work for what he gets, Claude believed. A man looking for a hand out, was no man at all.

Claude went upstairs and brought Laverne a glass of warm milk. He had found a few of the leftover sleeping pills back in the corner of her medicine chest, and he gave her one of those as well.

He was used to rising at 5, so there was no use in trying to go back and finish his sleep. Besides, it probably made Laverne a little more secure with him sitting in the living room while she tried to doze off again.

He knew there was no real danger, at least not right now. He had 2 champion hunting dogs that slept on the porch. If someone set foot on his property, or one of the sows got loose, they'd raise a ruckus. The dogs were great for geese and ducks, but they also announced strangers with great enthusiasm. Plenty of time for him to grab the shotgun within arm's reach.

Daybreak found Claude putting on his overalls, ready to go down and tend to the hogs. He ran the Farm himself. God had never seen fit to give them a child, but they accepted that, as His will.

They had about 40 Berkshire hogs, plus a few other mixed breeds. He liked the black and white "Berkshire" breed best. Their temperament allowed him to "free range" them most of the time. This type hog weren't the ones who looked to escape, they were well treated, and fed. Claude walked the fence line daily, looking for breaks or downed poles, anyway.

He had added some chicken wire to the fence line because of the goats. If not, they'd turn their head sideways to get at the grass on the other side of the barbed wire, then get stuck, not knowing to turn their heads sideways again to get out. Once they started struggling, they could get injured pretty badly. The chicken wire fixed that.

He liked "free ranging." The animals liked it too. It was more like they lived in the wild. A small stream ran through the acreage which kept them watered. The natural aquifer relieved Claude of having to water them himself.
There were several shade trees scattered around to provide shade on those hot summer days, as well.

A free range farm was simply less work for Claude, and resulted in more well-tempered animals. He didn't have to keep to a feeding schedule, or anything like that, just protect the animals from themselves and the elements.

The two times he had to be most careful was dead winter, when there wasn't enough forage for the goats, and the hot summer, which affected the hogs, and their weight, which determined their value at market.

The hogs' food supply, consisted of a diet of corn, corn cobs, and tons of table scraps. He had connections with two local cafeterias. The owners would either give, or cheaply sell, leftover or stale food which had to be disposed of. Uneaten bread rolls were the hogs' favorites. Claude never used meal, or packaged food. The merchants who bought his animals could tell the difference in the meat, and paid more per pound for that distinction.

These last few days, Claude had been more and more concerned with Laverne. Those hellish dreams she had. Was this the third December she'd experienced these nightmares? He couldn't remember.

Maybe Old Doc Dufort could refer them to a specialist. The last time Claude had brought it up to her, she'd put her foot down and refused to go elsewhere, or even to discuss with her doctor, any such a referral. He brought the option up to Laverne, again with the same results.

"They'd just start talking about me in Church, and in the grocery store," she said. "It would get out that I'm crazy, or addled, some people still say that lunacy runs in my Family. They always said my momma was a witch. I couldn't live with the town talkin' about me that way."

He'd tell her, "You need help, Laverne, I love you." But, she wouldn't hear of it, and demanded that he drop the subject. She was adamant.

Claude just shook his head in sympathy, and brought it up no more.

Ten

Travis Bayne figured that this Sunday was the day. Every soul had it's day of reckoning. For Chester and Eunice Tate, today was the day, or at least it would begin today. The child pornography had been the deciding factor. Christmas was just around the corner, he needed to be moving on, anyway.

At 2:20, Travis heard the grumble of the Ford pickup coming up the gravel driveway, the Tates, getting home from church. He stayed in the barn to wait. He laid on his bunk, eyes closed, on his back. Baiting the trap.

About 20 minutes later, Chester told his wife, "I'm goin' out to see how Tim's getting on. He'll be happy we're havin' fried chicken tonight, it's his favorite."

Chester knocked on the door out of politeness, but there was no reply. He peeked in and saw his farm hand laying on the small bunk, the blanket pulled up to his chin. Chester walked across the straw floor toward the bed, "Tim, you OK?" And he started walking towards him. When he got about half way to the bed, the floor suddenly gave way, with Chester falling into a hole dug over five feet deep.

The pain shot through him like nothing he had ever felt. After the first ten seconds the shock wore off, and Chester's last sight was the sharpened spears of wood which had been embedded in the ground, and now impaled him through the thigh, stomach, shoulder, everywhere. The "dead fall" that Travis built did it's job extremely well.

He closed his eyes, still breathing. He tried to cry out, but that hurt too much, and something was stuck in his throat. He heard, and felt, dirt being shoveled into the hole on top of him. It was light no more, and he couldn't breath. His mouth was filling with soil. It was getting dark. Chester heard him say, "This is for the kids on your computer, you sick son-of-a-bitch."

Travis quickly filled the hole with the dirt he had been hiding under an old tarp in the corner, and put a deep layer of straw over the fresh grave. No one looking in the barn would see anything out of the usual.

Travis stripped the bunk, and wiped down anything he might have touched, even though he always wore his work gloves, even to bed. He threw all the linens and his blanket into the wood stove, and lit two pieces of hardwood with the kindling he had brought down from the house earlier.

In about ten minutes he walked inside the main house and went into the kitchen. "Chester said he'd see you in a bit," he told Eunice.

Eunice turned from her deep fat fryer and said, "Why don't you sit and take a load off till he gets in. You know we always eat early on Sunday. And take off those gloves, work time is over." She turned back to the chicken.

"Almost," Travis said under his breath. He came up behind the woman and hit her square on the head with a crescent wrench he had in his back pocket. He didn't want to kill her, just knock her out for awhile. Then, he got busy. He brought his tools with him. Travis was always prepared. Eunice awoke to see Travis sitting across from her, eating fried chicken, biscuits, and gravy at the kitchen countertop. She was gagged with a sock in her mouth and what felt like duct tape wrapped around her head to secure it. The woman was flat on her back on her very own kitchen table. Each of her four limbs had been similarly taped to the legs of the table. She could move her head, but just a little. The daylight was fading, she had been out for awhile.

Travis looked up and smiled. "There you are, I was hoping you'd come back soon. Good chicken." He was still wearing his gloves. "Chester won't be joining us, he's gone away. But you'll have company soon enough."

She saw some blood on her dress and was frantic. "No, that's chicken blood," Travis said. It's not your blood, I didn't try to kill you, just wanted to knock you out for a spell. "No, I put all the leftover gizzards, liver, necks, you know, stuff we don't eat, all over the kitchen and screen porch, and doused you with chicken fat and blood. By the way, that headache, you're missing an ear."

"Then I cut holes, big holes in the screen porch, and latched the kitchen door open so the wind wouldn't accidentally close it. The animals will smell that for miles around, and come for their supper. Once they eat all that, maybe a day or two, they're gonna get hungry, again. Then they'll come calling on you. Those kids on your computer, this is for them."

Travis left a couple of lamps on, and walked out of the house. He had an old suitcase with some of Chester's clothes, a pair of shoes, toothbrush, and razor with him. He tossed the cardboard suitcase into the passenger seat of the old truck, went back into the barn and threw the work gloves into the wood stove, which was really burning well now.

Travis felt high, again. Maybe this was the best one yet. What was this in the past three+ years, 10 or 12 people? All dispatched with alacrity and style. How more would flush his prey toward him. At least that was the original motive. Now, maybe he liked it two much. He and Lester agreed on that. Maybe it was the thrill of the plan and the kill, not revenge, but Travis still held to his values.

He had one more link to cut, and it would be easy. He remembered the Address of "Earl the Oil Man." It was directly on route #613, between Moss Point and Pascagoula.

After dark, Travis drove the F-150 and parked it about ¼ mile from Earl's place, off the road, behind a couple of trees. He waited an hour to get acclimated to his surroundings. No traffic passed, no dogs barked, but he had been trained to take nothing for granted. Travis unscrewed the interior dome light, and slipped out of the cab of the truck.

With him he had a noise suppressed Glock 19, 6 ounces of C-4, and a mercury triggered detonator, all courtesy of "the man," several years ago. He stayed in the cover provided by the bushes for the entire approach, arrived at garage side of the house. There it was. The oil truck, parked beside the house. Tomorrow would be Monday.

Travis approached the house, no lights on, no TV playing, and no dog, which is why he brought his Glock. He quickly shaped the charge, under the oil tank, but close to the driver's seat to make sure Earl was a goner, and ever so carefully secured the detonator beside the charge, inserting the metal leads into the plastique.

Tomorrow, when Earl hit the first bump in the road, the mercury would complete the circuit, and the whole tanker would go up in a ball of flame. Most likely, it would be blamed on spontaneous combustion from fumes inside the container, or secondly, Earl's reckless handling of a cigarette. Ironically, the extra 10% Earl had been shorting his customers would come back to bite him in the butt.

As a safety, anybody Earl had talked to about "Tim" would start looking in Meridian...perfect. Lester would be proud. Travis backtracked to the truck, even more slowly than he had approached. Once there, he took highway #613 to Pascagoula, turned off on Cedar Street till the dead end, which had long ago, been surrounded by boarded up homes.

He slowed the pickup to about five miles per hour, put it in neutral, and jumped out, backpack in hand, just before the truck hit the Pascagoula River. The splash was a quiet one. He jumped behind a bush, and stayed still on alert for witnesses. There were none. Lucky them.

He waited. Only ten feet off the bank, the depth of the water would envelop the entire truck. He checked before, it always flooded here. He watched until the cab was completely submerged, then turned back toward highway 90, and headed west.

Eleven

Tuesday, two days later, Travis was sitting at a local breakfast place in Pearlington, Mississippi, almost to the Louisiana state line. He had spent Monday night in a hotel in Biloxi, home of the newest set of casinos in the country. The place had been filled with tourists and strangers nobody paid any attention to.

It was the "Holiday" season. What better way to celebrate than to come down to the coast and lose next month's house payment at the blackjack tables? It was strange to Travis what people did for entertainment. Cheap drinks, cheap rooms, cheap everything, until you added up what the trip really cost. They don't build these big casino hotels because the odds are in the gambler's favor.

He had set out early that Tuesday morning, catching a ride on a moving van at 5:30 am. It was headed west on 90. The trucker had taken this slower route because of a girl friend he was going to see on the way. Travis mentioned to the driver he was meeting his brother and the rest of his family at the eatery, so the driver politely declined Travis' offer for breakfast. Besides, he wanted as much time with his "friend" as possible. Travis couldn't help but notice the white circle around the driver's left ring finger. Did she not know, or just not care?

At the diner, Travis bought a local newspaper. Page 6 of the Gulfport, paper described a "Blazing Inferno," near

Moss Point, in which the driver of an oil truck, Earl Bunch, had been killed. The causes were unknown, but the authorities said foul play was not suspected.

That last line made Travis smile. He paid his check for a "Country Boy Special" which consisted of two eggs, toast, grits, sausage patties, and coffee, black. He left a tip that was appropriate, not to be remembered as too big, or too cheap...not to be remembered at all.

He walked out into the parking lot, breathed in the early morning air. It was clear, crisp, and clean. He knew it was going to be another good day. He started walking, heading west. It was good to be alive.

Twelve

It was a beautiful Sunday in San Antonio. There was less than a week left until Christmas, and the weather was in the mid-60's. Toni, Rhonda, Tom, and Rosa, were at Rosa's house having Margaritas, Coronas, chips with salsa & guacamole dip, as their favorite NFL team, the Dallas Cowboys were beating up their arch rival, Washington Redskins. It was a rout, 27 – 3, in the fourth quarter. It was in Dallas, under the new dome which Jerry Jones had built.

As the Washington quarterback threw his third interception of the day, Tom said "That should finish any hope the 'Deadskins' had. I'm going back to check on the girls." With that he set his beer down and walked back to the girl's domain, which used to be a playroom when they were smaller.

He found Maria, now seventeen years old, and Anna, fourteen going on twenty five, scanning through the teen magazines and searching the computer on line for their favorite stars. Currently it was Justin Bieber.

"Hey girls, what's up?" he asked. He had been around them enough to know that they were at the age when he was only occasionally "cool" to be around. They loved Tom, who had been filling the void as their male role model. Their deceased father was KIA in the middle east had not wanted to desert them, but such was war. Tom was special to both girls, but they thought he had no idea of what was really happening in the world. Among their peers, adults were all clueless.

Today's stars, Lady GaGa, Justin Bieber, and the rest of the young clan had already surpassed Paris Hilton, Lindsay Lohan, etc. who they considered to be old news. They humored Tom and dropped some names, just so he might know who the next big hit, or sensational star would be. He mostly just listened, and nodded.

Tom thought he remembered when he started liking Elvis and the Beatles. That was a long time ago. He still felt allegiance to George Jones, Loretta Lynn, and some of the "old timers," but that was in the past. A beautiful, more refined past, but the past, still the same.

Tom made some small talk, just enough to show his interest, then smartly did what grown-ups should do at this stage in a teenager's life, turned and left them to their own teen-age world.

He was walking down the hall, back toward the butt-kicking the Cowboys were dishing out to Washington, when his cell phone started vibrating on his belt. "Oh no," Tom thought. "Another weekend emergency, just what I need."

But, when he pulled the phone out of it's holster, the caller I.D. started with "985" Who and where was that? And then he thought, my second cousin Claude, in Slidell. He answered, "Claude, how you doin?"

His cousin seemed startled. "You cops have all the latest gadgets, don't you? Next thing I know, you'll have one of those 'Dick Tracy' wristwatch communicators."

Tom laughed. He had never been particularly close to Claude, but family was family. And if he was calling, then something was amiss. "Tom kept it light for now, "No the readout on my phone said 'dumb red neck' and you're the only one I know."

Claude lowered his voice conspiratorially (even though he wouldn't know the meaning of that word), "Can you talk for a minute?"

"For you, anytime." Tom answered. "It's, Laverne," Claude
said. "What's wrong with her?" Tom asked. "That's just it," Claude said, "I don't know." He talked softly, almost whispering. "Something's wrong with her." Tom walked into the kitchen, to talk, the game noise was getting louder, as the Cowboys scored again.

Claude told him about the nightmares Laverne had been having, getting worse the past three nights, now. "It's happened around the holidays for the past couple of years, but this time it's worse, and she won't hear about going to the doctor. She said last night she saw a man walking toward her. In the background was a big truck with a very fat man inside, burning out of control. She can't describe the man coming toward her, just that he has eyes like pools of fire."

"How can I help," Tom asked. "I've got some vacation time coming. You need help with the farm? It's only about 600 miles there. And, I might know a doctor who could give you a reference."

"No, no, the farm's never been better, and she won't see no doctors. I just thought you might have heard some police chatter about something, you know, something close to that burning truck image she has in her head."

Tom finished, "In that case, you let me make some calls.

I'll do whatever I can from here, anything to help you and Laverne. And, Claude, you did right to call me, but you keep that farm buttoned up, stay alert. They always said Laverne's momma had the 'sight', you pay attention."

"We're fine here," Claude assured him. Between the dogs and my Winchester, we're fine. Ain't nobody getting close to us without me knowing in advance.

Tom had Captain Daniels on his speed dial. Out of respect, and protocol, he motioned Toni into the kitchen. He explained the situation with his cousin. Then said "Daniels knows people in Louisiana, he went to school there." But I didn't want to call him without asking you.

"Do it!" Toni said, "Let me know how I can help." Toni left the room, giving Tom privacy to talk. Tom reached the captain right away. Daniels was happy to help, saying he would call his contact with the State of Louisiana in Baton Rouge, first thing in the morning.

A couple of hours later, Toni and Rhonda had said their goodbyes. The girls were getting ready for bed, it was a school night, after all. Tom and Rosa had settled in, Rosa was curious about what clandestine happening was afoot. Tom proceeded to tell her about Claude's call, Laverne's visions, and also about Captain Daniels promise to look into the matter.

"I just wish I knew what to look for and where to find the answer," Tom lamented. "Maybe Daniels will find something useful."

At just that moment, Maria walked in with her favorite "movie star" decorated robe on, to say goodnight. It was a tradition. You didn't go to bed without saying so, especially with company in the house.

"Look for what?" Maria asked. "Nothing," Rosa said, "Cop stuff."

"Mooooom," she said in three syllables. "You know I can find anything...It's called Google." Rosa looked at Tom with her eyebrows raised, "She's right, you know." Tom nodded to Rosa, "If it's alright with you, let's try it." Rosa said, "We can use my laptop, it's faster."

The three of them hurried into Rosa's guest room, which doubled as an office. Rosa sat in front of the computer screen whose background was appropriate for San Antonio, a large photo of "The Alamo."

"No mom, I can make it search faster." Rosa looked at Tom, "She's right again," and gave up her chair to the girl. Maria clicked the icon for Google, hit "advanced search," and began. "So tell me what we're looking for," Maria said, "and keep it as simple as possible."

Tom started. "There was a fire in a vehicle, where someone died." Maria looked at Tom like he was clueless about computer searches, which he was.

Maria, "When?"

Tom, "Recently."

Maria, "Where"

Tom, "Possibly Louisiana, probably the southern U.S."

Maria, "What type vehicle?"

Tom, "A truck, possibly a 'big rig"

Maria, "Anyone hurt?"

Tom, "A man died, burned to death, probably the driver."
Tom added, "He could have been fat."

Maria, "Fat won't help, anything else?"

Tom, "Not that I could recall."

Maria typed in "November, December, fire, driver, burned, killed, truck, rig" and hit enter.

In .22 seconds, there were over 7.4 million results, sorted by how many of the key words were in the news story. Maria sat back in her chair. "Let's look at the first page, that's usually what I do." Tom wasn't going to argue. About halfway down the page, there it was:

The Mississippi Press
Pascagoula Ms.   Tuesday, 12/14/2010

Local man killed in tanker accident. Earl Bunch, 46, of Moss Point died when his oil tanker exploded, early in the a.m. hours, Monday morning. Mr. Bunch, Owner of Earl's Oil Delivery L.L.C., had just begun his rounds, delivering oil, when the tanker he was pulling exploded into a blazing inferno. No cause for the explosion has been determined, but the Mississippi Highway Patrol, and the Moss Point fire marshal have ruled it a probable accident. Sherriff Will Perkins of Moss Point was quoted as saying that Earl was a constant smoker...

Tom and Rosa were stunned! Maria, and a now, a peeking Anna, thought it was no big deal. Any teenager could have found it. Tom asked Maria to print the article, and she did. Next, he called Captain Daniels and left a voice mail. He asked that Daniels hold off on making that call to Baton Rouge. He would explain, tomorrow, in the office.

Tom sat down with his head in his hands, wondering what to do next. First, Tom thanked Maria. She had done the police work that would have taken months, years ago when he first came on the force.

Rosa thanked Maria, herself, and then sent the girls on to bed. She and Tom reviewed all the occurrences and data they had reviewed. Tom finally said, "I've got one thing left to do.

He looked at the clock. It was 8:30, Sunday evening, but Claude was his cousin. He sat down and called directory assistance for Moss Point Mississippi. After telling the dispatcher he was a detective from the San Antonio Police department, he was connected to the home of Sheriff Will Perkins,

Sheriff Perkins answered his phone himself. After apologizing profusely for bothering the man on Sunday evening, Tom explained that it was a family matter he was trying to clear up.

He asked a few non-pertinent questions, and expressed sorrow for the loss of Mr. Bunch. Finally, he had to ask the one thing he really wanted to know... "Sherriff, not to be indelicate, but was Mr. Bunch a heavy man?"

Perkins answered quickly, "No he was not," Tom glanced thankfully at the kitchen ceiling, but then the Sherriff added, "He was downright fat!"

Tom thanked the man for his time, and immediately called Claude Thibodeaux. Tom said, "I'll call you in the morning, Claude. It's probably nothing, but load the shotgun, and keep it close."

Thirteen

Still heading west on U.S. highway 90, Travis walked off the early morning breakfast He had just been on the road for an hour or so when he had to make a decision. It was his first *Situation*, in the last couple of days.

Here was the metaphorical and physical "fork in the road." Highway #190, bent right, northwest, toward Slidell, Lake Pontchartrain, Interstate 10, and New Orleans. Highway 90, veered southwest, taking a much more rural path, connecting to New Orleans via the old Fort Pike Bridge. Coming into the city as the Chef Menteur Highway.

The past couple of years, he had travelled the southern route. Today, Travis decided to take the #190 toward Slidell. More people, less noticeable, and maybe more action for his tour. It was also much easier to hitch a ride toward a larger town, and eventually New Orleans. After only a few minutes, a truck towing a trailer stacked with cut pine trees stopped to give him a lift. The driver wore a red flannel shirt.

His name was Clete Boudreaux, and Travis Bayne realized he was entering "Cajun" country again. The dialect and the names left that unquestioned. Mr. Boudreaux was on his way to the lumber mill, just outside of Slidell, and "could use the company, someone to chew the fat with," he said.

Travis introduced himself as Jim Mason, from Houston. "Mason" was now wearing jeans, with an Atlanta Braves ball cap, and t-shirt, under his back pack. He spun his yarn about the Merchant Marines, again. Living on a ship, learning how to fix things. He had just used it, but those tracks were dead, literally, and it was one of his most favorite facades.

Travis was talkative. He wanted to get his story out there for examination. One of the few times a man can have a long, uninterrupted conversation, with few questions asked, is when he's the passenger, and the roads are narrow.

He elaborated that he was heading for Baton Rouge, to see family, and hoped to pick up some temporary work, before getting there. It wouldn't be right to show up at their front door with his hand out. Finally, Boudreaux asked, "What can you do?"

Travis smiled, and replied, "Just about anything. Farming, plumbing, carpentry, painting, just hard, honest work with no complaints...you name it."

"Well," the driver mused, "let me take you by the mill, that's where I was headed, anyway. I 'spect they could find a place for you. At least for a while. Most people today think they're too good for hard work, rather live off the government tit."

It was another twenty minutes of twisting roads but they made the drive safely. Once at the mill, Jim (Travis) was introduced to the supervisor, a man named Mr. Rosette. He was a small, skinny man but his handshake was that of a man who had spent plenty of time working in the mill. Here was a working supervisor. He had a pair of jeans on, covered in sawdust. A blue bandana hung around his neck, catching the sweat as it trickled off his head.

Rosette explained that there were many facets of the lumber business and this mill, but his plant's main purpose was to make utility poles from yellow pine stock. They supplied poles for power and phone companies all over the state. They did some pulp and paper production, but most of that was done in their Bogalusa mill, about twenty five miles north.

Rosette offered Travis $8 an hour, cash, off the books, to be a "fill- in", that is to do whatever they needed each day. The supervisor said that they would run short of men loading pine stock when multiple trucks came in, and occasionally needed electrical or plumbing repairs, which at just the $50 service call, ate into their profits.

"I figure you can save us some money, which means a bigger bonus for me," the little man explained. "Also, we've got a "bunkhouse" in the back you can use. Don't have to worry about your belongings. Every man has his own locker, and his own lock.

He looked straight at Travis and stated, "Any man caught trying to steal around here, can kiss his ass goodbye, and I'm not talking about the law arresting you," he said flatly. "We mind our own business. What you do on weekends, is up to you. While you're on mill property, you follow our rules. Any questions?"

This setup was perfect for Travis. Off the books, strict rules, Monday through Friday, perfect. But, he thought of a couple of questions anyway. "How about food, where do we get it?" Rosette replied, "We have a meal truck, comes by three times a day. Or, you can buy some supplies in town, and use one of the two ovens in the bunkhouse to cook with. Most use the meal wagon, give it a try. And on the side, if you feel like you need something stronger than alcohol, I can provide that, too, for a price. Got some good meth, cooked it up myself, and I'll sell it to you on credit."

"I'm not sure about that stuff Mr. Rosette, but I do have one question." Travis asked. "Sometimes, because I spent so much time on ships, I guess, I start to feel 'cooped up', you know, the walls closing in. Is it all right if I spend some time outside, maybe sleeping under a tree, or taking a walk at night?"

Rosette smiled, for the first time Travis had seen, "Long as you're here at 8 am, sober and ready to work, I don't care what you do after 5 o'clock. Just don't go out partying, and drag your ass in late to work. At 8:01, you don't work here anymore, understood?" Travis nodded that he did, and Rosette continued his spiel.

"But," he stressed, "it's starting to get colder at night, so take advantage of that 'pot belly' stove in the bunkhouse, when you need to." There's no shame in taking cover when mother nature decides to make a change.

Travis held out his right hand, and said, "I think we'll just get along fine. Rules, I can handle, so long as they don't change." Rosette grinned again, "They haven't in 50 years, and I doubt they will on my watch." I'll get your locker set up, and issue you a hard hat and gloves. You won't last a day here without work gloves. Travis always liked the "gloves" part.

They shook hands, and the supervisor had another man, an old black man, named Otis, show Travis the layout of the mill, bunkhouse, lockers, restrooms, and break room. It turned out that Otis, used to be the "do it all" person. He was a genuinely likable man, and knew the mill operations backward and forward. He'd just gotten too old to do anything requiring physical strength. The mill kept Otis employed to run errands and such. He was family...been there for over 40 years.

During the next few days Travis exhibited a variety of skills, fixing a leaky roof, stopping a plumbing leak, but mainly using 'elbow grease' labor, loading and unloading pine logs. Of course, what he as really doing was reconnaissance. He kept his mouth shut, and his ears open. He was friendly, but rarely initiated a conversation. Otis gave one piece of advice to Travis,

"You stay away from that shit he's peddling. Some men have to turn over half their check each week to pay for their habit. I hear his wife sells it too, to some of their friends, probably finds it's way to the schools too." Travis nodded, thanking the man.

The hard labor kept him in shape, and even better, you didn't have to think to do this job. Yes, if Travis were in the 'saw cut rooms' he had to be extra careful and alert due to the danger involved. That was infrequent, so he had plenty of time to think ahead. Maybe he'd just work here for a while and move on. He didn't need the money, but it didn't hurt. He'd decided to wait for the right opportunity to get some real money, either here or at his next stop.

He walked the dirt roads almost every night. Each recon showed him a different side of the area, it's roads and infrastructure. One night he learned where the supervisor lived, as he passed a small ranch style house, set off the road by only about a hundred feet. The brick ranch had a neat yard, hedges trimmed, and the boss's silver Dodge Ram truck parked in the oyster shell driveway. L. Rosette, was painted on the mailbox, letting the whole world know that this was where Mr. Lawrence Rosette, mill supervisor of the largest employer in Slidell, lived with his wife of 22 years.

There were no toys in the yard, and no swung set. This confirmed what Travis had heard, no children, living. One had died of pneumonia, before he reached the age of 6. That had been about six or eight years in the past. The Rosettes had not conceived another child. Oh well, you gotta go sometime, he thought.

Behind the house seemed to be hundreds of feet of dense foliage. The ground was not cleared or otherwise tended to, what today's environmentalists would call "green space."

Night after night, Travis walked, explored, and occasionally searched for a possible mission. One night, he walked a new route onto South Military Road. The night was moonless, he was in his element, operating in the shadows.

Moving slowly and looking closely, he could just make out the presence of a house. It was completely dark, and was set back 500 feet from the road. The house seemed to be swallowed by the huge property on which it sat. He could see a barn, but no other structures. "This could be the one," thought Travis. The mailbox said "Thibodeaux." That name stuck in his head. He didn't know why.

The setting was remote, with no nearby neighbors, but it was only about fifteen minutes from the mill, maybe ten at a double time pace. He decided to check it out.

Slowly, he moved up toward the house, choosing his path carefully, to remain unnoticed. One step every five seconds or so. Stalking, and staying invisible. When he was still less than half way, he heard a hog snort, then another. This was followed almost immediately by the unmistakable baying of recently awakened hunting dogs.

There were two of them at least. "Shit," Travis thought, he was downwind. Downwind was sloppy, he knew better. Don't get careless, Bayne, he told himself.

The dogs could smell him. He froze for five minutes, ready to run if things got louder then even more slowly, retreated to the road and turned back toward the mill. The ruckus was still going on as he was walking slowly, innocently, down the road. This wouldn't be easy.

Fourteen

Laverne Thibodeaux sat straight up in bed screaming, "He's here, he's here. Claude, get the gun." Claude grabbed his Winchester and walked out to the front porch, flipping on all the exterior flood lights, front and back. The dogs were still barking furiously, but stayed on the porch. He heard hogs snorting in excitement. Claude walked into the front yard, panning the yard, until he got to the fence around the hog pen. There, he spotted a pair of eyes, staring right at him. Yellow eyes, just like they were on fire, reflecting the security lights in the blackness. He took another step, and suddenly the raccoon scurried back to the safety of the nearby barn.

Claude took a deep breath. The dogs stopped their howling, the hogs were still restless, but were beginning to settle down. False alarm. False alarm for two reasons. He had seen the raccoon, and the flood lights were wired to motion detectors. If anyone had come within fifty feet of the house, they would have come on automatically.

He went back into the bedroom to reassure Laverne, telling her about the raccoon. "No," she said emphatically, "It was him. He was here. No doubt about it. What I saw was no critter with a ringed tail. It was a man. A man with fire in his eyes."

"Laverne, the flood lights didn't come on, and the dogs stayed on the porch. What happened was the raccoon upset the hogs, then the hogs got the hounds all riled up, so they automatically started making a commotion. It was just a chain reaction." "No," she repeated. It was him. He's here, and someone's going to get killed because of it."

Claude pleaded, "Let's go down to New Orleans for a few days. A change of scenery will do you a world of good. We can stay with cousin Bessie. She's always inviting us down. That big house she lives in has three, unused bedrooms."

Laverne looked at her husband. "No, we're safe here, now. I can feel it. No need to leave. Besides, who'd mind the farm as well as you?"

Fifteen

As Travis was walking down the road, away from the Thibodeaux's house, he saw the flood lights come on. Then he saw a large man walk out into the yard with what looked like a shotgun. The dogs were still barking. They could be heard for miles, Travis thought. "I've go to be more careful," he said to himself. "Damned downwind...how stupid can you get?" The "not easy" thought had solidified into impossible, or complicated at the very least. He decided to pass this situation, and wait for something better.

The next few days were routine. Travis was feeling that he had been lucky...he had picked the wrong target. He had no intel on the house, didn't know there were dogs, a man with a shotgun...what was he thinking? He knew that only one step followed unprepared, and that was failure, which in his case meant death.

One morning, the mill boss was giving Travis some instructions on his workload for the day, when the office manager, a woman named Blanche, came into interrupt. "Mr. Rosette, I'm awfully sorry to interrupt, but it's you wife on the phone, again. She says that clothes dryer is making the same racket again, and Sears can't come out till Monday."

Rosette scowled, "As much as we paid them the last time, it ought to work forever."

Travis saw his opportunity. "Sir, maybe I can fix it. I'm good with motors and the like, maybe I can save you some money." With this idea the boss brightened up. "Tell you what, Mason, after work, you ride home with me and look at it. If you can fix it, I'll add four hours to your next payday, and a home cooked meal. If you can't fix it, no hard feelings. How's that sound?""Great," Travis said. After 5, I'll wash up and be ready to go in ten minutes. Rosette added, "I'd like to keep this between us. I don't want the men thinking I'm playing favorites," he said, looking directly at Blanche.

"Works for me too," Travis agreed. "OK," the boss said, at 5:10 you start walking up the road, north. I'll finish up and leave here at 5:15, pick you up on the way home."

Rosette said to his office manager, "Call Darlene, tell her to keep the appointment with Sears, we can always cancel if Mason here is successful. And tell her to set an extra place for supper. You could use a home-cooked meal, I bet."

"That's more than generous." Travis smiled, perfect he thought. Everything went according to plan. After Rosette picked up his employee, it was only a short, five minute drive to his house, the same one Travis had walked by, days earlier. They walked around to the back door and entered through the "mud room" which was where the cantankerous appliance was kept. It was an old Kenmore, sitting beside a washer of the same brand and vintage.

A woman walked in and extended her hand to Travis. "Darlene Rosette," she said as an introduction. She turned to her husband, "Hi, Larry, I heard you drive up and thought you might be back here."

Ms. Rosette was skinny like her husband, had short salt & pepper hair pulled back into a bun. She didn't see much of the outside world, her pale complexion was evidence of that.

Inside the laundry room was a pile of tabloids, including *The National Enquirer, The Star, The Globe,* etc. Travis guessed she was addicted to all the various soap operas, game shows, and probably Oprah, as well. She was the type to leave the TV on at all times during the day, reading the movie "rags" while watching the tube. Travis hated this type of person...a consumer. Someone who took up space, used air, and gave absolutely nothing back in return.

Travis rose, introducing himself with his pseudonym, "Jim Mason, ma'm, pleased to meet you. Can you show me how this dryer is acting up?"

She turned the knob to "spin dry" and the commotion began. The vibration was loud and getting worse. Travis knew immediately what the problem was. "Alright, ma'm, you can turn it off now."

He asked Rosette, "Do you have a pair of pliers? Not too big, but I think I can fix her up."

"Come with me, out to the tool shed," Rosette answered. "You can pick out what you need."

"Great," Travis thought, "another chance to recon the property." There were two outbuildings. The larger one was a detached garage. Possibly large enough for a small car, but probably housed the meth lab. The second was an 8 x 10 prefabricated shed, which had an orange power cord running to it from the house.

The two men walked to the small shed, and Travis saw that it was neatly kept and organized. He immediately saw the pliers he needed, but scanned the walls, looking for anything which might serve his needs later.

Travis pointed out the tools he might need, and asked Rosette if he could bring those inside. He had left his gloves at the mill. It would have looked like overkill, to bring along a pair of rough leather gloves to look at a simple problem. He'd have to remember to take care of any prints on his next visit.

Back inside the mud room, Travis and Rosette pulled the dryer out from the wall. Travis slipped behind the machine and popped the motor access panel open.

As he suspected, there was an axel hex bolt which was loose on the wheel, which made the drum spin awkwardly. Every time she had turned it on, it vibrated, and loosened even more. He worked his hand with the wrench up inside the machine, located the bolt, tightened it, and removed his hand. "Please try it now," he asked Darlene.

She turned it on, and this time it was smooth and efficient, hardly making a sound.

The Rosette's were beaming. Travis and his boss pushed the dryer back into place, careful not to crimp the flexible exhaust pipe, and the job was complete.

"Well, it's too early for the supper I owe you, but we could sit outside a spell and have a cold one," Rosette suggested. "Darlene, here, has fixed a country ham, and we can eat in about 30 minutes or so. It'll take her about that long to get the mashed potatoes and red-eye gravy ready.

"As long as it's the back porch," Travis replied. "I noticed a bench, and a lot of trees back there. I'm really a nature lover, at heart." Of course his real motivation was twofold, not to be seen by passing traffic, and to further recon the foliage and undergrowth behind the house.

"Sure, the boss said. And I can show you how far back our acreage goes while it's still light out. We even have a cold spring on the property."

As it turned out, the acreage was left natural. Rosette was no farmer, didn't like animals, and was married to his job at the mill. The land he owned had a single path from the backyard to the property line. The lot had a road frontage of only 250 feet, but was 700 feet deep.

Even with closer neighbors than Travis thought was ideal, the backyard was only 50 feet from the natural foliage. Once you crossed the yard, no one could see you.

Travis was good with foliage.

The two men walked the lot, all the way back to a small stream. The landowner pointed further into the undergrowth and boasted, "My property goes all the way back to the county right-of-way, just 50 feet from the #190 highway. The property line's about fifty feet further than where that big Live Oak stands. I'm hoping somebody will come along and want to open a 7-11, or put a truck stop there. Then I'd be sitting pretty."

More useful information.

About that time, they were called into supper by Darlene. Travis asked if he could wash his hands first, as an excuse to see more of the house. There wasn't much to see. He walked down the hallway past the bathroom, and got the general layout.

The Master bedroom with it's own bath was located at the end of the house. Off the hall were two smaller bedrooms and a hall bath, which he hurriedly used to wash. He was careful not to touch the faucet or doorknob with his hands, where prints could be found, and he strolled back to the dining room table.

The ham was tasty, it was "honey cured" and much better than some of the salty ones Travis had eaten in the past. He took his time, chatting about his "family" in Baton Rouge, and his time in the Merchant Marines.

After the meal, she served pecan pie, with coffee, which happened to be Travis' favorite dessert. He said his goodbye's and although his boss offered to drive him back to the mill bunkhouse, Travis declined, explaining that a good walk would allow him to work off the calories from the "wonderful" meal they had provided him. He actually wanted to go around to the rear of the property, to see if there was anything there which might compromise his future actions. He had made up his mind that this opportunity was just too good to let pass.

Travis circled back to highway #190, through an open field that probably grew soybeans in the season. Once he was directly behind the Rosette's property, he saw there were no stores or gas stations, and very little traffic.

Two more days at the mill, and it was finally Friday. At quitting time, Rosette handed Travis his weekly envelope, with the cash inside for his labor. Travis folded it up and stuck it in the back pocket of his jeans. "You know," said the supervisor, "you're the only man I've ever had, who didn't count the money in front of me to see if it was the right amount. And yes, that something extra we discussed about fixing the dryer, is in there too."

Travis smiled, with his "good Travis" face and looked at the ground as if he were embarrassed. "It's not about the money, boss. It's about doing the job the right way, no matter what you're doing. That's what I'm all about."

"Well, we need more men like you. Then this country wouldn't be in the fix we're in," Rosette said, turning to walk away, he looked back and said, "Have a fun weekend, Jim, see you on Monday."

"Thanks, I will," said Travis, and he whispered to himself, "and I'll see you before Monday."

Sixteen

After dark, he went off the mill property to a spot about seventy five yards from the main road. The spot was marked by three, good sized stones, and it was here that he had buried his backpack the first night he was at the mill. He had wrapped everything in oilcloth and cellophane, in case of heavy rains, but there had been none. Better safe than sorry, he knew.

Travis recovered his pack, which included his Browning, a silenced Glock, KA-Bar combat knife, a few remaining ounces of C-4, some timers, and extra ammo for the rifle and Glock. The Glock ammo was 9mm Hydra-Shok.

With this brand the bullet entered the body the size of a dime, and when the hollow point mushroomed, it exited leaving a hole the as large as an orange. Guaranteed one-shot stop, in the hands of an experienced shooter like Travis Bayne. In combat, you didn't want to give a dying enemy time to take the extra shot.

This was his "Travel kit." He had hidden other caches of para bellum (for war) equipment at locations spread around the country, along his usual route. He had a large supply of such ensconced in a small cave in west Texas. What he had here, with him now, was more than adequate for this mission.

He approached the house by cutting across the same deserted soybean field as before, entering the Rosette property about 50 yards deep into the undergrowth. He took his time moving toward their backyard, and once there, sat a few feet deep in the overgrowth and waited. He knew that under normal circumstances, 2 a.m. was the low point of awareness in the human body. He would wait until 1:00, these people went to bed early.

Travis slipped the latch on the screen door, smiling as the kitchen doorknob twisted open in his gloved hand. The He slipped the latch on the screen door, smiling as the kitchen doorknob twisted open in his gloved hand. The entrance wasn't even locked.

He walked down the hall to the Master bedroom. He had noticed a squeak in the hardwood floor near the hall bath, when he had washed up the other night for dinner. When he came to this part of the hall, Travis spread his feet as wide as possible, walking right on top of the floor joists...no squeaking there.

He had decided to make this as simple as possible so he entered the bedroom quickly. Husband and wife were both sleeping on their backs, the man was to his left. Travis backhanded Lawrence Rosette hard on the temple, with the butt end of the KA-BAR. He'd be out for a while. He then placed his gloved hand over Darlene's mouth, and shook her awake. Her eyes were as big as saucers.

"No one has to get hurt here," Travis said. "I want to know where he keeps the mill cash box. Then I'll tie you both up and leave." Travis figured as much cash as the boss was paying out at the mill, meant he had a stash somewhere. A stash Rosette wouldn't want left at the mill for the weekend. He had never seen a safe in the office, just a metal box, usually tucked in Rosette's bottom desk drawer. "After the money," he said shoe me the drugs, yeah, I know about the meth business you have going."

Travis was always amazed at how cooperative people became when they thought they were going to live. Just give them the money, and they'll go away, was the mentality.

With his hand still over Darlene's mouth, she led him across the bedroom to the bathroom. Behind the toilet, was a small section of tile, meant to look like a plumbing access. Darlene pointed to the tile and nodded. "You get it," stated Travis, "and quietly." Darlene slid a box and a bag of meth out of the hiding place, and handed them to him. "You face the shower while I check it out."

He looked inside and was satisfied that this was the mill money, and the drugs. Travis put his right hand on her chin, his left on the back of her head, under the "bun" of hair, and spun it, quickly hearing the expected "snap" of her cervical spine. Darlene would bake no more pecan pies, Travis thought. What a shame. She made good pie.

Now he turned to the real work at hand. First, he gagged the man with a sock, securing it with duct tape. He then used plastic flex-cuffs he had purchased at Wal-Mart to bind his feet and hands to the bed. Travis then began to wipe the kitchen down, saw that there were dishes in the dishwasher, which probably included those from a couple of evenings ago. He loaded the appliance with liquid soap, and turned it on full. No prints anymore. He went to the mudroom, and with Windex and a rag in his gloved hands, completely wiped down the dryer, and since he was there, the washer, the door, and the floor as well. He left nothing to chance...that was for the losers in life.

Travis went out to the tool shed and grabbed a pulley he had seen during his previous trip, along with some rope, chain, and an open Master lock. He dragged this collection of items through the path in the back of the property, and dumped them at the base of the large live oak tree. Now, back to business. He walked back into the house, down the hall, into the Master. The injured man was starting to move. His eyes were still closed, but he saw the man's eyes fluttering under his closed lids...no matter. Travis cut the flex-cuffs with his knife which only freed Rosette for a second, as he removed the man from the bed, and re-cuffed him again.

Bayne grabbed the cuffs securing the skinny man's ankles and dragged him out of bed, making a thump like a sack of potatoes hitting the hardwood floor.

He dragged the man down the path, feet first, until they reached the large tree. Travis went about his work, ignoring the semi-conscious Rosette. In about thirty minutes he had rigged the pulley up to one of the larger low limbs of the live oak. That limb was about twelve feet off the ground. He further secured the man's feet with the chain, and hoisted Rosette up in the air to where his outstretched hands would still be a foot off the ground. He secured the man's hands to the ground with flex cuffs attached to an auger he had screwed two feet into the soil. Travis peeled back the duct tape and momentarily removed the sock from his boss's mouth.

Rosette had become more aware, almost entirely awake. He saw the cash box and bag of drugs down on the ground, and snarled at Travis. "When I get out of this, I've got friends. Friends who really know how to use a circular saw and a plane. You're going to be sorry. Sorry and skinless, you SOB."

Travis smiled, "What you don't understand, Larry, is that this isn't really a robbery. I just needed the practice. Being a drug pusher, just made you pay." With that said, he saw Rosette's expression change quickly. He stuffed the sock back into his mouth, reinforced the duct tape so that it wrapped completely around the man's head. Then with a one inch flick of the wrist, he cut through Rosette's jugular. Lester whispered "*The ear*" and Travis cut off the left ear, and walked away. He left the meth lab for the cops to find.

Travis took his backpack, and the cash out of the box, with his hands still gloved, got the Ram's keys off the hall table and drove the truck two miles back to the mill, parking it in it's usual place. He put the bag of meth under the driver's seat.

He walked about a mile up the road before he made his way through another out-of-season field, on the way to Highway #190, South. He got to the highway, and immediately crossed over to walk toward the oncoming traffic. The last thing he wanted right now was a ride with someone who could ID him at this spot and time.

In two hours he had covered about twelve miles. He crossed the highway, and waited for a ride. Baton Rouge, hell...he was going to the Crescent City.

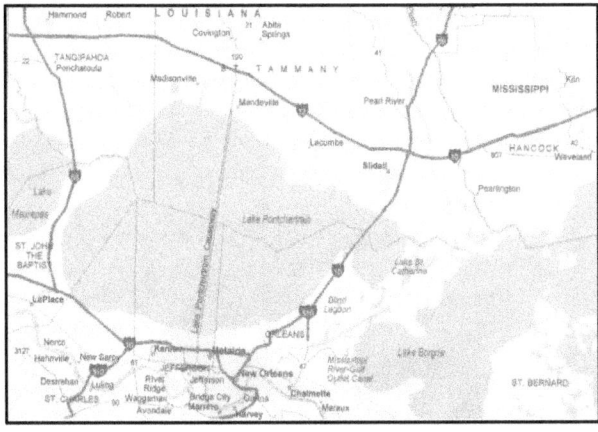

Seventeen

Jimmy Wilson had worked for Sears almost eight years. He had held several positions with the giant retailer, but for the past three years had found a home in the appliance repair department. With times being tough, new sales were down, but repairs were double last year. It was hard to keep up. He had not liked his scheduler putting the Rosette's dryer repair off until Monday, but they were swamped with jobs. Jimmy's cousin still worked at the mill, so he was tempted to come over and do the job on his own time, Saturday. But, the 4-year old had the flu, and Jimmy's wife Tina, was a Pentecostal, and wouldn't hear of him working on the Sabbath.

He drove the repair truck up the long driveway, got out and rang the bell. No one answered, but that wasn't so unusual. Darlene Rosette had been one of Jimmy's junior high teachers, and had told him that if arrived while she was at the grocery, to use the key under the flower pot. He located the key easily, and came in the front door. "Sears repair" he called out, but no one answered. Oh well, Jimmy had been here several times before, and knew right where the dryer was located.

He set down his tool belt and turned the dryer on to observe the problem Darlene had described. He was amazed. It ran like it was new. He turned it off and on again, three times, same result. Well, he shrugged his shoulders and put his tool belt back on. He went to the kitchen to write up a repair invoice, for the service call, but decided not to charge them. The Rosettes were good people. Instead he walked to the hall table which held a "scratch pad" and phone, to write them a note.

What was that smell? Jimmy definitely detected a strong odor similar to sewage and waste coming from the bedroom. Jimmy called out again, "Anybody home?" all was quiet. As he got closer to the Master bedroom, the smell grew stronger. As we walked in he saw an empty room, with some plastic connectors on the floor. The smell was unbearable, He put his hand up to cover his mouth and nose, identifying the bathroom as the source of the foul stench.

Her head twisted to look backward to him, Jimmy still recognized a bloated Darlene Rosette, whose body was leaking fluid out of every orifice God had given her, and some that he hadn't.

Jimmy was sitting on the front porch steps when the two State Police cruisers pulled up, lights rolling, sirens wailing. Right behind them was the chief of police for Slidell, Lou Burnside. He was a solid investigator, and a cousin of Lawrence Rosette.

After the officers confirmed what lay inside the house, they secured the home with crime scene tape, and sat beside a shaking Jimmy Wilson as he went through the chain of events that led things to this point. He repeated it several times, to several people, telling the same story every time. He was quickly eliminated as a suspect.

Chief Burnside had called the mill. He had been told by Rosette's secretary, that her boss's truck was in the same place he always parked, but no one had seen him since quitting time on Friday. She promised to call if he showed up. Burnside wasn't putting much stock in the probability of that happening. Whether Rosette had killed his wife, or had met a similar fate, he wasn't going to walk into the mill anytime soon.

Two more cars arrived, this time from the police department. The boss told them to stay out of the crime scene, and search the property for clues. Ten minutes later, a young officer named Guilotte, found a big one...hanging from a tree behind the house. They gathered around the body, averting their eyes. "Looks like he bled out, chief," Forcet said. "I'd like to cut him down, but forensics would have a cow if we screwed with the scene."

"Fuck forensics," Burnside yelled, "the man's part of my family. Take some crime scene photos with your cell phones, or if you have a small camera in one of the vehicles, that would even be better. And don't touch him after he falls, but for Jesus' sake, cut him down."

The officer cut the rope, and Rosette fell like a stone, his back snapping like a dried tree limb.

Chief Burnside went back to the front yard of the home, pulling his cell phone out as he made his way toward his car. "Chief, one of his officers yelled, you might want to see what's in the garage."

He walked in and recognized the set-up for the manufacture of crystal methamphetamine. I thought he was out of that shit, he told himself.

He needed something to lean on while he called his friend, Mayor Stan Wallis.

After a couple of minutes the mayor was on the phone. "Sorry, Lou," the mayor apologized. "I was in a budget meeting, but Janet said it was an emergency, and you don't use that word lightly."

In the next few minutes the chief described the scene which they had found. The condition of the bodies made him believe that the murders occurred two or three days ago, even though he admitted, he was no coroner. The experts would be brought in for that. He also told the mayor about the drugs.

"He was formerly a user," the law enforcement man said. "I thought all that was behind him. But murder is murder, and I don't want the drugs getting in the way. He was family, and I want it investigated.

The scene surrounding his cousin's death, and the way the body was arranged, made him feel they were after a vengeful madman, or a hunter.

He was right on both counts.

"I want Baton Rouge in on this," said the mayor. "You know how I hate it when those LBI assholes get involved, but we're going to need the help on this one. And you being kin to the victim, it keeps us in the clear regarding the investigation."

The Mayor said he would make the call to the governor and attorney general, right away. They had the responsibility to direct the Louisiana Bureau of Investigations. The Mayor hoped they'd listen. They didn't need the appearance of a conflict of interest.

Eighteen

It was Tuesday night, just after shift change, and Tom Granger had heard nothing more from his cousin Claude, in Slidell, about his wife's visions and nightmares. He decided to call. It was the right thing to do.

Claude answered, and after a cursory, "how you doin' buddy?" from each, the conversation moved on to Laverne and her dreams.

"It's the strangest thing," Claude said. "One morning she woke up and said 'we're safe, nothing to fear', and we haven't lost any sleep since. Hell of a thing though. A big load off my mind, but, you know, we had us quite a double murder scene here in Slidell, yesterday."

Claude went on and explained about the murder of the Rosette's, at least what he had read in the local paper. He told Tom about the man hanging upside down, to bleed to death. He said the man's wife had died of a broken neck, but not from a fall, not an accident.

Claude said the family was fourth generation Slidell people. Well respected. Church going folks with no apparent enemies. "Well," he concluded, "I guess that they had at least one."

Small talk ended the conversation, with Tom saying how relieved he was that Laverne was doing better. He hung up with Claude, and called Rosa. He needed help putting some pieces together.

"Could I come over for a bit? I've got something I want Maria to look up for me, with your permission, of course."

Tom went on to describe his conversation with Claude, and the recent events which had taken place in Slidell, mostly in general terms.

Rosa didn't want her seventeen year old daughter to start having nightmares either. But, Tom had a hunch. And his hunches were usually worth a second, or even a third look.

"It's up to her," Rosa said. "Maria will be eighteen next year, and wants to study computer science with a minor in criminology when she goes to college. I think she'll be interested."

Twenty minutes later, Tom's pickup pulled into Rosa's driveway. Maria was eagerly waiting on the living room couch. Tom asked Maria to excuse them for a moment, so that he and Rosa could discuss the situation in more detail, before getting Maria in a situation which was horrifying, at best.

Tom explained the situation in Slidell. He pulled no punches, "It's gory, it's madness, all done by a sick person, so don't be shocked. Pretend it's a crime novel, and not real people involved."

Maria went to Rosa's computer, and with Tom and Rosa looking over her shoulder, and logged onto Google. The two adults were amazed at the amount of information which existed for a crime which happened only yesterday.

Maria put in the key words, Slidell, double murder, and Google exploded with information about the crime.

Slidell Sentry News
Tuesday, January 11, 2011

Man and wife brutally murdered at home. Authorities searching for leads. Robbery not deemed a motive.

The story went on to the bare facts, the names of the victims, Rosette, and that they had been killed sometime over the weekend. The way the bodies had been discovered by a repairman was mentioned. The state of decomposition of the victims had also leaked out to the media. Thankfully, the Sheriff had not allowed the press to photograph the remains.

There was also a TV newscast about the crime, posted by WWL-TV4, the CBS affiliate out of New Orleans, again with no film or images of the victims. Slidell is close enough to be considered part of the New Orleans viewing area.

The basics of the case were pretty close to what Claude had described to Tom. Tom looked at the crime through the eyes of a hunter, and a cop. After a few minutes, Tom said, "I've seen enough." I've got to call Toni. He got his supervisor on her mobile phone on the first ring. "Toni, I need to call the sheriff in Moss Point again, Tom declared. "There's something to this that just stinks."

He explained that there was no direct linkage to the two crimes, and no similarity, either. A man killed in a truck fire. A driver, who was a known cigarette smoker, working around fuel oil. The other case was a man and wife, brutally butchered at their home.

The only link, were the dreams of Laverne Thibodeaux, and the instincts of Tom Granger.

Toni gave her OK without thinking twice. It was out of their jurisdiction...way out, but Tom had a keen sense of putting pieces together. Besides, it was just a phone call.

Thankfully, this wasn't a late Sunday evening call as had been the case previously. He called Sheriff Will Perkins office and was put through to the man after only about 30 seconds.

"Sheriff, I'm the one who called you about the fuel tanker fire. Again, I apologize for calling you at home that night on a Sunday."

"I had a feeling I'd be hearing from you, again," Perkins stated. Tom was shocked at his comment. "And just why's that, Sheriff?"

Perkins decided to play "cat and mouse" with Tom, and asked the $64,000 question. "Well, Detective from Texas, why did you call?"

Tom recovered his pace in the conversation, asking "After that fire a few weeks back, was there anything ever tied to the victim, Bunch, I believe was his name?"

Perkins didn't answer, but asked Tom another question. "You a hunter, detective?"

"Not as much anymore, the job and all, but yeah, I hunted deer every year until about four years ago. Joints got achy, work got longer, and I got older, not necessarily in that order, but I spent some time on hunting leases with my friends. Why do you ask?"

"Same for me, the sheriff replied, but here's why I ask. Two weeks after that fuel oil explosion, we found us a couple of dead bodies out on a farm. It was a married couple, no kids. Murder is something we don't have much of here, and the State people rationalized it as some crank head, out of his mind on crystal meth, looking for a quick cash score."

"But you don't buy it?" Tom asked rhetorically. "No chance," Perkins said. "These were honest, church going people, with no money. And the way they were killed, leaves me know doubt." Tom questioned, "How's that." Perkins elaborated,

"The minister from their church found the bodies, at least he found the woman's body. They hadn't shown up for church on Sunday. First time they'd missed service in years. But, the reverend thought, everybody gets sick, and with the flu going around, he figured they didn't want to take a chance on giving it to the whole congregation. Then, they missed the second Sunday in a row, and he decided to pay a call on them at home, after his noon sermon. Are you sittin' down, detective?"

Tom lied, and said that he was. "The woman's body had been secured to her kitchen table with duct tape. The coroner from Pascagoula said she'd been eaten alive by wild animals. There were no big bites, like a bear or anything. He thinks she lasted three or four days like that. The back of the house had been left wide open. Even the screen porch was cut out."

Tom was trying to erase the scene from his mind, but was having no success. "What about the husband?" Tom asked Perkins.

"Well," Perkins began, "his truck was gone, and some of his clothes, razor, and toothbrush were missing." I didn't buy that easy way out. I called Hank, one of my hunting buddies, and had him bring his hound dogs over. We gave them the scent from some of Chester's dirty laundry, by the way, it was Chester and Eunice Tate." Tom interrupted, "What do you mean?"

"Their names, were Chester and Eunice Tate," said the sheriff. "Sorry, sheriff," Tom said, "my head is spinning." Perkins came back, "No apology needed, so's mine. Anyway, the dogs come, and I'm ready to search the whole farm acres for the man. But all of the dogs ran immediately to the barn. Then they started whining, scratching the floor, and everybody is staring at each other. The Pascagoula coroner, the three highway patrol officers, my deputies, and me. The barn was empty."

"Then, my friend Hank spoke up and said, 'I think he's under there,' pointing at the dirt floor. "Now, we had a crime scene set up. I hated to interfere with anything. Jackson was sending down a forensics team, they'd be there in four hours. But, what if he was buried there, and somehow had enough oxygen to live? We started digging. After about a foot, the stench was so bad even the coroner was giving up his lunch, outside, of course."

"He was dead?" Tom asked. "For several days, the sheriff said. He fell into a dead fall that had been dug out and concealed in the floor. His body weight impaled him on spears stuck into the ground, sharp side up. And he didn't die right away. He had dirt in his lungs. Someone trapped him, and buried him alive."

"Sound like some 'crank-head' to you?" There was no verbal response from Tom. "Me either. Sounds like a hunter. A person who hunts other people, and enjoys it."

"Then, I read about this thing in Slidell on Monday. I'm bettin' it's the same man. Sounds like a pattern. I'm no criminologist, barely made it out of high school, but I know people, and I believe that sounds like the same killer. If we can prove that it is, then it's the F.B.I.'s problem. Once you cross state lines, they get involved, but I'd like to catch him locally. Avoid all that jurisdictional B.S. over interstate flight."

"I'm going to fax you all my notes on this, said the lawman from Mississippi. But you should know two things, one, I tied him back to a connection with Earl Bunch, the oil man, and two, he's headed your way. Now if I can get your fax number, in about fifteen minutes, you'll know all that I know. Or at least all that I think I know."

"All I ask, is that you keep me in the loop on this. I'm taking it personally."

Tom promised he would. He gave Rosa the gist of the conversation. She commented, "If we'd looked back a couple of weeks afterward, and followed up on the oil truck explosion, we'd have known."

"Couldn't have prevented it, though. We wouldn't have tied the two events together, except for the second killings in Slidell." Tom gave a reassuring look to Rosa, and headed for his office to review the faxes which would be waiting for him. Once he got there and compared the Moss Point case with what little he knew of the Slidell murders, he was as convinced as Sheriff Will Perkins, that the two were linked.

Tom read the sheriff's notes. The interview shed light on the killer, he read each page three times. Sheriff Perkins had made inquiries around town, asking about anyone noticing vagrants or druggies hanging around. He got zero. His, was a quiet, rural speck of a town where everyone knew everyone else, and they all watched out for their neighbor. Perkins could use this to his advantage.

He got nowhere with his investigation, until one morning when he was having breakfast at "Waffles and Dogs," a local breakfast and lunch place. The sheriff had boldly written at the top of an 8 1/2 x 11 lined page, **Notes Below:**

Jan. 14, 2011, 7:20 am, I saw Fred Flowers come in for his usual breakfast. Flowers walked over to me hanging his head, the way many of our citizens had lately. Fred owns the local hardware and paint store.

I invited him to sit, while his food was cooked

Flowers stated his sympathy for the recent murder victims, Chester and Eunice Tate. He elaborated that it was a shame, especially now that they were making good progress at the farm, with his extra help and good weather. After all, Flowers filled orders for Mr. Tate almost three times a week, now.

I asked Flowers what help he was talking about. The rumor was that his son had run off with a waitress, and hadn't been seen for weeks. I asked Flowers if the son had returned.

He answered in the negative. He said that Mr. Tate had hired himself a "farm hand," who could do just about anything which needed doing.

I asked, and he answered that he had not seen the man, but had heard he was formerly in the Merchant Marines. He claimed to be headed to his brother's car business in Meridian.

I asked how Chester had found this man, want ads, a relative's friend?

Chester replied that, coincidentally, as he put it, they had connected through Earl Bunch, who had picked the man up hitchhiking. He said Earl dropped him off at the Tates during his service call there to refuel their oil tanks.

He said helper's was Turner. To his knowledge, no one else in town had seen him.

He then asked what had happened to the farm hand, was he dead too? I was halfway out the door, already.

Sworn affidavit from Fred Flowers, owner of Fred's Hardware and Paint, attached hereto.

Note: to anyone reviewing this file. My conclusion is that the farm hand killed the Tates, and then eliminated the only person who could identify him. Inquiries of a car business owned by a "Turner" in Meridian, proved fruitless.

Nineteen

The next day, Tom requested a meeting with Lieutenant Toni Ramos, and her boss, Captain Daniels. The meeting began at ten o'clock sharp in Daniels office.

Although Toni knew of the conversations Tom had with the Moss Point sheriff, he had not told her anything about the details of their discussions. Tom had the floor, and proceeded to outline the story and conclusions, he had drawn which matched the discussion with the Moss Point sheriff.

Toni and Captain Daniels both read the conversation notes taken at the chance breakfast meeting and subsequent interview.

Daniels finally broke the silence. "So what's our interest in a couple of murders in Mississippi and Louisiana? What do those crimes have to do with the San Antonio Police Department? I know they were horrific, seemingly without motive, and possibly, just possibly, connected. What business it of ours?"

Toni looked at Tom. She got it. "Tell the man," she said.

"He's headed right at us," Tom said. "And, if we can tie this up a little tighter, maybe he can be stopped before he gets here. We just need to establish a connection. Then maybe we can predict what path this man will take from here. I know it's not much to go on, but sometimes we get so tied up in arrests that we forget that crime prevention is supposed to be part of our job."

"I called the chief in Slidell last night. It was late, but the couple killed there were relatives of his, so he was happy with any clue, any place to begin. I gave him the facts of the Moss Point case, and he promised to have all of his men conducting interviews today. He's calling me this afternoon at 4 pm."

Daniels looked at Toni, "It's your man. What do you suggest we do?"

"I think we should be up here in your office at 3:55, waiting for the speakerphone to ring," Toni said flatly.

It was agreed that the call would be transferred to the Captain's office. After informing Police Chief Burnside that he was on a speaker phone, Tom would lead the discussion from this end, as he was the only Texas cop who was familiar with the murders in Moss Point and Slidell.

They kept themselves busy for the rest of the day. Time seemed to drag on forever for Toni. Tom looked at his watch so often, he felt the hands were moving backward. Luckily it was a slow day at Police Headquarters on Nueva Street.

Tom delved into some old cases, mostly halfheartedly, until he finally decided that he had so much on his mind that he was doing disservice to anything else he reviewed. He had a thought, and immediately went down to the I.T. department.

The department head, Pete Moore, was eating breakfast tacos at his desk, the office door wide open, when Tom spotted him and came to his office. Pete was a short, heavyweight man, probably 280 pounds, and getting bigger every time Tom saw him. He was now up to three full chins.

"Just gettin' a late breakfast," the man said. Tom doubted that. Here at 10:30, he was probably eating his second or third breakfast. Pete washed down the last bite of the taco (there were four empty wrappers on the desk), threw his garbage into the wastebasket, and said, "Tom, how can I.T. help you?"

Tom pulled up a chair, to make the conversion somewhat more intimate. "The captain, and Lieutenant Ramos are working on a project. We need a couple of hours of your help, no big deal, but the meeting's at three today (he lied to give himself time to spare) so we need your best person.

Tom was becoming more political and less blunt in his approach. He knew some name-dropping would help him get results.

They think a killer has been working the Gulf Coast states for a while now.

That got Pete's attention. "You mean like The Taker?" he asked. Pete had helped in that investigation.

"No, and if you can believe it, this killer is terribly worse." Tom told him about the two cases under review right now, in order to give Pete an idea of what they were looking for, and added, "We think he's traveling close to the water, maybe along I-10, or there about. He hunts his victims, and kills them in their home. The cases we're looking at now, have both been rural, man and wife, no kids at home, but brutally murdered. We know of these two, we're hoping to fill in the blanks. It would help if we could find similar crimes.

"Yeah," Moore said, "I could try to see what comes up on a search like that. I could hunt for double murder, terrible slaying, butchered, all kinds of key words. I can access LexisNexis, and all the search engines. What time did you say you needed it?" Pete Moore was all about politics. "Oh yeah, 3 o'clock, you'll have something by 2:30, just be sure I get credit."

Tom assured him he would, and walked back to his office to wait some more. This was his least favorite part of the job.

Tom went out to his favorite delicatessen for lunch, killing time. The location was close, 715 S. Rio Grande, just a few minutes walk. The place was named *Shilo's*. In a town where over 50% of the residents had Hispanic roots, *Shilo's* was the best German deli Tom had found. And, that included the two years he spent in Germany while stationed there in Uncle Sam's Army. He had even picked up a little of the language, which made him more welcome in Germany, and even more so at the deli.

"Guten Tag," Tom nodded to the hostess, she smiled and reciprocated. He wandered over to his favorite corner table, which was saved for him until two o'clock, every day. This was old world courtesy, and it made him sad on the days he couldn't make it in for lunch.

One of Granger's rules was to always sit facing the door. This is where he had sat the first day he came, and almost every other day since then.

Tom had the bratwurst, red cabbage, and German potatoes. It was great food, but he still caught himself glancing at the clock every couple of minutes. Watching it isn't going to speed it up, he thought. His mom had always said "a watched pot never boils." There was wisdom in those words.

All through the meal he was chiding himself for this latest inquiry. Trying to connect two crimes, both out of his jurisdiction...hell out of his state! What was he thinking? Getting Toni, and now Captain Daniels involved. All because of his cousin, Claude.

He'd be the laughing stock of the station, just when he was getting everyone more comfortable with his leadership.

How foolish. He sat there just shaking his head. The waitress came over, "Mr. Tom, is the food bad?" she asked. He was startled, "No, nein, die essen, ist sehr gut." A smile returned to her face as she placed the check on the table. "Danke," he said, left a generous tip, and walked out the door to return to his "mess" he thought.

He had been back in his office only a few minutes, it was only 2:15, when he saw the butterball figure of Pete Moore rumbling toward him. He was clutching several pieces of paper, and had a smile as wide as a Halloween pumpkin.

He barely fit through Tom's door, closed it behind him and blurted out "There's lots of them, and recent too." Tom cleared his desk, and they went through what Pete had brought him. He had used the key words in some of the on-line search engines, just as Maria had. The advantage the I.T. department had was that they had access to more than just Google, and could be much more through with their search. The first sheet said:

Gadsden County Times

Tuesday, October 19, 2010

Quincy, Florida... Local man found decapitated in home, head missing. "A hideous, gruesome scene," said Gadsden County Sheriff Roy Pickett. The victim is believed to be Oliver Bray, age 62, a lifetime resident of Quincy, and owner of Bray's Dairy.

Moore placed the second story on Tom's desk. And, if possible, it was worse.

Defuniak Herald

Tuesday, October 26, 2010

Defuniak Springs, Florida...Search party finds missing couple...crucified! Brad and Colleen Branson were discovered in a forest, yesterday, large nails attached their bodies to trees. The forest is located on the Branson property, itself, comprising almost 200 acres. The couples apparently bled to death over several days, from the nail wounds and animals feeding on the bodies, according to the county coroner. A

reliable source stated, "It was like a crucifixion. I'll have nightmares for the rest of my life. Blood was everywhere."

Tom picked up the phone and called Toni's office just across the hall. He had seen her playing the "waiting game" as well, when he returned from lunch. "Can you come over? It's big."

Less than a minute later Toni was reading the press excerpts from the first two cases. Pete Moore was close to his third heart attack. "Sit down, Pete," Granger warned. "You're getting too worked up. Here, give me the pages, you'll get the credit, don't worry."
Toni Ramos and Tom Granger stared at the next story, it was no less painful.

The Daily Review
Wednesday January 20, 2010

Morgan City, Louisiana...Couple killed in home. Lyle and Emily Forcet were discovered dead, in a bloody heap, inside their small home in rural Morgan City. Police spokesperson, Lucille Ponder, released some details of the crime.

Ms. Forcet died of a broken neck and back, and was "scalped." Mr. Forcet had all four limbs broken in several places, and a hatchet driven into his skull. He was missing his left ear "The entire kitchen was like a slaughterhouse," Ponder stated. "The police will use all our resources to find the person who committed this hideous crime."

The two cops sat down with a sigh. "We can't spring this on Captain Daniels at four o'clock." Toni stated the obvious. "Let's call him, and go up now." she said.

There's one more, The I.T. man said, and the way the hits were coming in, I might have more to add to the stack in an hour or so. They decided to read the fourth story, before calling the Captain.

The Gonzales Inquirer
Wednesday, February 17, 2010

Gonzales, Texas, Two brothers were brutally murdered, on their ranch. The men were Samuel and Jed Cummings.

They were both hanged from a large live oak tree in the back of their 125-acre ranch. Texas Rangers discovered the bodies after complaints from neighbors that there were dozens of vultures feeding on something in the trees. Authorities close to the crime said the men were alive when hung, as there necks were not broken.

"So, they were eaten alive?" Toni asked, the horror evident on her face. "Yes," Granger said. "There's no doubt in my mind that we're talking about the same killer. Gonzales is only an hour from here. He was probably in San Antonio last February. Let's call Daniels. He needs to see this. You draw a line on a map, he'll pass through here at about the same time this year, mid-February. Toni called the captain, and asked to see him early. "The earlier the better," she begged.

Captain Daniels read the news reports while the two key members of his staff sat in front of his mahogany desk. They watched his expression turn from inquisitive, to concerned, to horrified. They noticed his color was considerably more pale, as he finished the fourth page.

He put his head in his hands, shaking it slowly, trying to comprehend something so horrible it could not be comprehended.

Toni broke the silence, "So boss, what do we do now?"

They bantered around a great many angles. The aspects they had to contend with were so diverse. After several minutes of heated discussion, they finally agreed on three things:

1) They would not speak to the Police in Slidell, in any detail, regarding these new connections. They would just see what he had found which might match the Moss Point crimes. They would tell him of possible FBI involvement.

2) The I.T. department would continue their search, but only for today. The SAPD homicide staff would have an all day "brainstorming" session, tomorrow in the Captain's conference room, beginning at 8 am. Daniels would ask Chief Bernardo's permission to have the FBI sit in on the meeting.

3) If the group came to a consensus that these crimes were committed by the same person, The FBI would to run the investigation. It was multi-state, and the bureau had the resources to do the best job. This information would be relayed to the local law enforcement communities of Moss Point and Slidell.

Toni got on the phone and asked the dispatcher to call the squad, Padilla, Jones, and Cheatham, and advise them of the early morning meeting. Tom glanced up at the clock. It was 3:50. The call from Slidell was due in only minutes. Tom noted, "If anybody needs to go, go now, we may not get another chance in the next hour.

No one did. The anticipation was building.

At 4:01, the captain's phone buzzed. He pushed the speaker button and heard "There's a call for Detective Granger from Slidell, Louisiana." Daniels had the call put through, Tom answering the phone. "Chief Burnside, thanks for being so punctual. You are on a speaker phone with my lieutenant, Toni Ramos, and Captain Daniels, if that's OK." It was, and the conversation began.

The Louisiana lawman answered, "First, I just want to thank you for calling me. We were at a dead end yesterday, and we've made more progress today, than we had since the crime occurred. We had gone over the crime scene twice. No evidence, the dishes had been washed, the appliances and floor in the laundry room and no prints at all, which tells me he wiped it down."

"But, thanks to you, we think we know who the killer is, or at least who he said he was. And we've got a pretty good description. He went by the name of Jim Mason. He actually was working 'off the books' for Mr. Rosette, who is the supervisor at the local lumber mill just outside of town.

We were interviewing employees at the mill and hit pay dirt. My cousin's secretary, Blanche said, that Lawrence and this Mason guy, were in a discussion when she overheard Mason say he could fix my cousin's clothes dryer. According to Blanche, she also overheard her boss offer dinner and some extra money to this guy.

That's why the Sears repairman found the dryer working when he got to the house. During the repair was when this Mason guy probably saw the layout of the house. What his motivation was, is beyond me. We interviewed every single employee at the mill. Everyone said that this man was soft spoken, and an extremely hard worker. I'm developing a facial sketch of this man, I'll send it to you. Oh, I almost forgot, they said he was just out of the Merchant Marine, headed for Baton Rouge."

Tom looked at the captain, and Daniels gave him the nod. "Chief Burnside, you'll probably be hearing from the FBI in the next few days."

"Why's that?" Asked the chief from Slidell.

Tom told him that this crime appeared to be connected to a series of grisly murders over the past couple of years. He added that Florida, Louisiana, Mississippi, and Texas were probably involved in this killing spree.

"I'm all for that," said the Slidell sheriff. "I hate to lose control, but I want to catch this bastard. You tell them we've compiled a very large amount of evidence and interviews, that they are welcome to."

The call was ended, everyone at the desk in San Antonio took a deep breath. "The Merchant Marine background, which is probably fake, is key. It's the same story he used in Moss Point," Tom pointed out.

"After tomorrow, we'll be out of it," Daniels said. "He's still headed our way," Tom lamented. "The good thing for us is, he likes small towns. But, then, he's very unpredictable."

"I'll make the call," Daniels said, "the FBI will be here in the morning."

Book Three

Twenty

At 8 a.m., the group was gathered in Captain Daniels' conference room. Chief Bernardo had invited the SAC of the local FBI field office, late yesterday. The FBI man attended the meeting, along with one of his top investigators. Daniels introduced the special agent in charge to the group as Bill Tillman.

Tillman was a big bear of a man, but not overweight. He wore a red and blue striped tie, and had an American Flag pinned to the lapel of his suit coat. Looked like standard FBI dress code.

Tillman introduced his associate to the group, and passed out both their business cards. Her name was Angela Davis-Leigh. She was an attractive black woman in her early 40's, a somewhat on the heavy side but carried herself well at about 5'10." She had a blue jacket and skirt, white blouse, and the obligatory flag pin, as well. Daniels then gave the names and rank of the SAPD group as well.

For the first hour they rehashed the four crimes which I.T. had uncovered by 3:00 yesterday, then an additional three, which had been discovered later on in the day. They added Fairhope, Alabama, plus Stowell and Brackettville Texas to the list. There were nine murder sites, if you counted the gas truck explosion separate from the Tate house. They had ten to twelve.

Administration had prepared folders for all those present which contained the media reports on the crimes, and had brought in a whiteboard to use as needed.

Toni took over the meeting. She turned to the group and asked, "Let's start with commonalities. Tom, you're close to this, what do you see?"He thought for awhile, then looked up. "Small towns, rural locations, close to the Gulf." everyone in the room was nodding as Toni turned to write this on the board. "Alright, anyone, what else?"

Billy Cheatham volunteered, "All the murders were on Tuesday or Wednesday." Davis-Leigh interjected. "Not true. They were all reported on Tuesday or Wednesday. The bodies were discovered on Monday or Tuesday and came out through the media the next day. To me, that shows that he's a planner."

"If you commit a murder on a Friday night or Saturday, and the victims have no kids you probably have until at least Monday to get a head start for your getaway. No mailman coming in noticing yesterday's bills still in the mailbox, probably no deliveries, or service calls, like the Sears repairman. By the time the bodies are discovered, he has had plenty of time to vanish."

Billy responded, "I can see that for the Monday discoveries, but Tuesday, let me see, yeah, in Gonzales and Morgan City the discoveries were on Tuesday. That could be cutting it close."

Starr Jones was working furiously on her Blackberry. She pulled up the calendar app. "No, she's right. The Monday before the Morgan City crime was discovered, was President's Day. People were off work, no mail, just an extended weekend. The Monday before the Gonzales discovery was Martin Luther King Day, with exactly the same effect, another extended weekend."

Toni looked around the room, everyone including a chagrined Billy, was nodding. She wrote the words "Smart," and "Weekend Killer," on the board.

Billy added another, better idea. "He's here in the late fall and during winter. All these crimes were between mid-October and mid-February, we have a time period encompassing only four months."

At that statement, Tom Granger's head snapped upward. "I told I.T. to check on the Gulf Coast. Maybe he just spends his winters here. The FBI man was writing furiously. He knew what this could mean.

Toni wrote "Winter" on the board. "People, what else?" The best evidence had been found in Slidell, so they started a recap of that crime. Tom stood and went over the murders and crime scene. He added, "We could get a composite sketch today or tomorrow. Are there any other questions?"

Starr asked a question she thought she knew the answer to, but asked anyway. "No prints in the house? He had dinner there."

Tom shook his head. "They went through the house twice. No prints, other than the Rosette's were found. In fact, he washed the dishes, and wiped the laundry room appliances and floor clean of prints."

Rosa Padilla had a flash. "Look under the dryer." Tom looked at her strangely. "Why?" She explained, "He probably had to pull the dryer from the wall to repair it. Once it was fixed, they pushed it back in place. Call the Slidell Chief. Ask him if they looked for prints under the dryer." Toni nodded, and left the room to call Louisiana. He returned in a few minutes. "He's going to get the crime scene people back out to the house, right away. He didn't know if they dusted under the dryer, or not." Now they had to wait, again.

Daniels offered an observation. "No pets were mentioned in any of the reports. Odds are this man stalks his prey, and none of the victims had dogs. I'd bet on it." Tom nodded. He has the instincts of a hunter. He smiled when he thought of cousin Claude's two prized hunting dogs. Maybe that had kept the killer away.

Everyone studied the cases, one by one, and reviewed two more. It was clear that they were fading. The group decided to take a one hour break, and have lunch brought in, afterward. Tom suggested *Shilo's*, he had a menu in his desk, and it was agreed.

During the break everyone was in their own business world, retrieving voice mails, texting, and calling in for messages.

Lunch arrived. They were all starved it seemed. The FBI picked up the check, which was a good beginning to the relationship on this case.

Tom was about to take his second bite of his Reuben, when someone knocked on the conference room door. An officer stuck his head in the door, looked at Tom, and told him he had a phone call from Louisiana. Did he want to take it?

Granger bolted out the door, Rueben in hand. He came back in five minutes and announced, "Bingo. Two prints under the dryer which weren't the Rosette's. They're trying to match them now."

Have him send copies to my office, today, said Bill Tillman. "Already done," Tom boasted. "I gave him your fax and email from the card you handed us this morning." With that, Captain Daniels asked SAC Tillman if he thought the FBI had enough to carry the ball from here. He answered in the affirmative, and the meeting broke up. As they were leaving, the group was strongly admonished...no press! This guy could probably disappear in a heartbeat.

Finally, Tom thought, a lead. A starting point. But to where?

"Captain, can I see you in your office for one minute?" Tillman asked. They both left the room as all the law enforcement people were collecting their material. Entering Daniels office, Tillman shut the door.

"I'm going to have to lean on you a lot, these first few weeks. Right now, your people know ten times as much about the crimes as mine, including me. If this guy is like we think he is, meaning a psychopathic man hunter, we've got no time to lose."

"We're here to help," Daniels assured him, not sure where this was going.

"I need one of your people," the FBI man admitted. "Only for two or three weeks, until we can get a handle on this."

Daniels knew that if SAC Tillman went to the chief, or heaven help him, the mayor, he would get exactly what he wanted. A mass murderer of at least nine people, on the loose. A sociopath who killed those people in a four month window. Was he working up north, in the summer?

"Who do you want?" Daniels asked. "Granger," Tillman answered. "He's spoken to the authorities in two of the murder locations, already. He speaks their "ole boy" language, doesn't talk down to them. That's important. These local cops get their back up, and get P.O.'d when my people, who can be a bit short at times, I'll admit, call and pull rank on them. Plus, he has the instincts of a hunter."

"Two weeks, and I'll have to clear it with the chief." Bill Tillman grinned, "Let me know if you have a problem and I'll have the DOJ call the governor." Here was the FBI, again, living up to their arrogant reputation.

Daniels handled the paperwork after meeting with the chief on the FBI's "request." He had promised Toni Ramos, that he would be more actively involved at her discretion, during the next two weeks. "Call me if you need me, don't if you don't, I'll stay out of the way.

Tom was enthusiastic about being involved, even though it would be short lived. This kind of case was right down his alley. Tomorrow was Friday. It would be his first day at the FBI building. He was due to help make a presentation at 9 am.

He was ill-prepared materially, and would have to "wing it" to a group of agents who all thought they were smarter than him. They can think what they want, I'll just give them their starting points. Locations, what to look for in their considerable resources, contacts, he had just received the facial sketch, before leaving the SAPD. He made twenty copies for tomorrow, and faxed over the sketch to the FBI. The composite sketch showed a white male late twenties to mid thirties, no beard or mustache, short hair, no piercings or tattoos, wearing an Atlanta Braves ball cap, and a pair of sunglasses. In other words, no one. The U.S. had just over three hundred million people. Of these, a little less than 50% were male, 25% of these, were either black or Hispanic, and according to the latest census estimates, 20% of the population fit the age range they had established. Tom's math showed that he had 22.5 million suspects. Great.

The next morning Tom was going to be in early. Tillman wanted to brief him at 8:15, before the presentation. Tom's cell phone buzzed. He looked at the number, it was from Slidell. Laverne he wondered?

It was the Police Chief, and he was hot. "I ran those prints through the NCIC (National Crime Information Center) database. I got a blank. A numbered and coded file #3826a41, with a phone number to call the CIA in Langley Virginia for all inquiries. What's going on? That database is run by the FBI.

Tom said, "Look, I'm on my way to meet with the head FBI man right now. They want me to liaison for a couple of weeks. I'll bring it up, first thing, and get back to you."

Tom drove into the visitors parking lot at the FBI headquarters, 5740 University Heights. It was a fairly new, but bland 4-story brick building. He could see where the terrorist barricades, and many other precautionary devices were placed. This was a result of Oklahoma City, and 9/11. He walked in at 8:05, a pass was waiting for him at the front entrance desk. One of the guards escorted Tom to the fourth floor, where he took a seat outside a closed door, in front of an obviously gay male receptionist. The door was thick, but Tom could hear yelling inside. In about two minutes a red faced man wearing a chalk-striped suit, burst out the door, not giving Tom a glance. Tillman looked out and saw Tom Granger waiting, minding his own business, and waved him in.

"It's usually not like this, Tillman apologized. Just hit a snag. Do you have any questions before we start outlining the presentation."

"You're reading my mind. The chief from Slidell just called. He ran the prints through NCIC. He drew a classified case file, with a number to call the CIA in Langley, Virginia. He got zero, nothing."

The FBI man put his elbows on his desk and leaned toward Tom. "I got exactly the same, and I called the assistant attorney general, and the assistant director of the FBI. They don't have enough pull to get that file. That's what the yelling you obviously overheard was about."

"I'll have to go higher up, threaten them with hindering an active mass murder case, etc., etc. And you know, Langley is 'spook city'. I'll have to start locking my doors at night." Tom didn't think he was kidding, either.

"Tell the chief, we've got the same problem, and we're on it."

Now, for the presentation. I had some of my admin people here all night creating a PowerPoint presentation. A color copy of it is in the file in front of you. Let's go through it and see what I left out. I also had the composite sketch enhanced, removed the ball cap for one example, the shades for another, and so on.

I also had some I.T. people review the nine cases we discussed yesterday, and come up with some uniform data for each case, age, race, gender, even dogs. Yeah, we made phone calls last night too.

Tom looked at the file, it was incredibly detailed. From what he saw, it was a much more polished presentation of the yesterday's SAPD briefing, containing all of the known facts, plus some other information gathered last night. The folder was blue, with the FBI seal centered right above the words, Privileged Information.

Tom thought for a moment that he could enjoy working here. The moment passed quickly, back to more reasonable thinking, and planning his first words at the lectern in eighteen minutes.

He went to the bathroom, and relayed to the Slidell Police Chief the information Tillman had given about the prints. "He's going higher up the chain, and taking some risks. I'll let you know when we make some progress."

That seemed to satisfy the chief. "One thing I forgot to tell you. Mr. Rosette was missing an ear. At first I thought it could have been a fox or a dog. But I talked to the coroner last night. It was definitely amputated."

Twenty One

Travis was on the move, again. He had spent the past couple of days in New Orleans' French Quarter. It was still several weeks before Mardi Gras, but there were plenty of people there. Most of them were from out of town, and almost all of them were either drunk, or high on drugs. He stayed away from most of the strip clubs, and drag shows, he jut wasn't into that.

The best parts of his stay were a beer and two dozen raw oysters he consumed at The Acme Oyster House. There were several more places with the same name scattered around the south, but this was the original, opened in 1910. He had rented a small room on St. Louis Street, but on the northwest side of I-10, away from the crowds. It was still only a 5-minute walk to Bourbon Street, but far enough away that he wouldn't have to put up with the non-stop revelry the Quarter was famous for..

Travis still had part of the rush he felt after the Slidell mission. He had seen a few people working there, but nobody really knew what he looked like. Since getting to New Orleans, he had swapped to the obligatory "Saints" ball cap, which made him blend in with the tourist crowd even more.

This morning he caught a ride on South Clearview with a delivery man driving a blue van, and crossed the Mississippi River over the ancient, Huey Long bridge. The trucker said that he was only going to Avondale, and the shipyards, just a couple of miles on the south side of the bridge, but Travis had said that was fine. He knew he had to cross, it was still highway 90, and you couldn't go over that bridge on foot.

The bridge, built in 1935, was over 150 feet above the Mississippi River. There were two very tight traffic lanes on each side, with two active train tracks in the middle. It was under construction for expansion, but the completion was still a couple of years away. This was perfect. Travis thanked the driver, and started walking west.

Twenty Two

It was a blustery, late December day in bayou country. Raceland, Louisiana was a peaceful, mostly white, but Cajun town of just over 10,000 souls. Situated in Lafourche Parish, it was the gateway to Creole America, along with nearby towns like Houma.

Working the oil rigs in the Gulf of Mexico, the shifts were mainly 14 days out, and 7 back home. The 7 days home were just enough time to visit a wife, a sweetheart, get drunk, and play a card game called Bourre (pronounced Boo-Ray). It was in one of these innocent card games that Marty Saucier found himself involved in this very evening, in a crawfish bar in Houma.

Marty was a wild soul. He loved women, loved to drink, and loved to fight. He was 27 years of age. At 6'2" and very well built he could hold his own in most of these Cajun bar fights. But this was Houma. He had few friends here, so he needed to win, and win honestly.

After more than a few Dixie beers, brewed in New Orleans, and a local favorite, Marty had run into a streak of bad luck. The last two hands, he had not taken a trick, and was forced by the rules to match the pot. One more of those, and his petite amour, Angelina, would not be receiving the bracelet Marty had promised her in the heat of the moment, only last night.

And he knew, a disappointed Angelina, was a cold Angelina. This was not an option he wanted to be saddled with for the next four days. He wanted to spend four days saddled, literally, with a happy, grateful, young woman. Marty had spent his first night back from the rigs with his wife, Bernadette, and their two girls...at least he thought they were his. After his first night home, he had made some excuses about seeing his co-workers at a retirement party for one of his crew, and dashed over to Angie's place in Houma. He had no intention of going back to Bernadette until the day before he was to catch the boat back out to the oil rig.

As fate would have it, his fifth card was trumped by the ace of diamonds, which meant there would be none for Angie. It took everything he had to match the pot, and out of cash he walked away. Saucier tried explaining to Angie on his cell phone, that he would make good in a couple of weeks, when he was on dry land again. But Angie's favors were in great demand, with at least three more beaus waiting in the wings, and the day was young.

Marty dejectedly drove back to his family in Raceland. He picked up highway 90, and took the highway #1 exit to his whitewashed home on Cypress St. It was just after lunch. The girls would still be in school. Maybe he'd get lucky.

When Marty Saucier walked in, Bernadette was surprised to see him. Marty was surprised to see Leland Bergeron lying in his bed next to her. His system went into immediate overdrive. He was instantly sober, and lit into Bergeron with all the wrath and fury he could muster, finishing the fight with an aluminum softball bat he kept under the bed.

Leland was trying to get his clothes on, and race out the door of the "shotgun" style house when Marty caught him on the kneecap with a violent swing of the bat. Leland's knee collapsed inward, but delivering the blow had caused Marty to lose his balance. Leland hopped out of the house while the staggering husband was trying to regain his footing. Marty heard the growl of a motorcycle which had been parked behind the house, out of sight, and raced to the front porch, only to see the interloper riding away, strapping his helmet on while trying to drive the Harley with only three working limbs. He was only doing about fifteen mph, but Marty was too exhausted to give chase. He threw the bat at the escaping man, but missed badly.

The neighbor across the street, an old woman named Hebert was standing on his porch, flipping the bird to Marty. He flipped her off in return.

He then turned toward the house. People were going to pay, and pay dearly. When he entered the house, Bernadette was holding a butcher knife in front of her. He went over to one of the kitchen chairs, righted it, and sat down in a slump.

"So this is what's been going on here, while I'm out working for a living?" he asked.

"No, only since you've been shacking up with that whore, Angie," she spat back at him. "You know what they say, what's good for the goose is good for the gander," she proclaimed defiantly.

Marty grabbed a cold bottle of Dixie from the fridge, sat back on his chair, and thought about the mess he had made of his life.

He didn't know how lucky he was, not to be named Leland Bergeron.

Twenty Three

The presentation began at 9:00, sharp. The conference room was about 1000 sq. ft., and set up with tables and chairs running parallel to the small stage at the front of the room. A screen for the presentation was behind the stage. Every seat was taken, with about thirty people attending. Agents were not drifting in, 5 minutes late. Tom figured when the SAC called an emergency meeting, people snapped to attention. Granger was sitting on the dais beside Tillman, Davis-Leigh, and two other men Tom had not yet met.

Bill Tillman rose to the lectern and asked for quiet. He gave the initial "good morning," and then the obligatory, "This is crucial, people. You must keep this information to yourselves. Absolutely no press. This will be a huge undertaking."

He then began outlining the case which had been thrust upon them yesterday.

"We have what may become the most prolific serial-killer in the history of our nation." That got their attention. "The reason I use the words 'may become', is that we have linked this suspect to ten cases in only 5 states, and we've only scratched the surface. I have agents who will be passing out the blue case folders. Do not open them until I tell you to do so."

The FBI man knew that once the agents started looking at

some of the gruesome crime scene photos, he would lose their attention for the rest of the meeting.

He gave them a moment to let this sink in, and introduced Tom Granger to the group. "This man made the initial connection between two separate murders, which shed light on what has been happening, right under our noses, for the past two or three years. Detective Tom Granger will be here to assist us, bring us up to speed, for a couple of weeks."

"He will answer to me, and only me. His job will be to inform us, liaison with the local law enforcement people where the murders were committed, and to use his instincts, that is, in determining whether he thinks a crime in another state belongs to this perpetrator, or not. I have assigned him a temporary office, down the hall from mine. Detective Granger, please." And he motioned Tom to the podium.

Tom walked to the microphone and began. He decided to try and "break the ice." He began, "I hate to be here this morning for two reasons. First, I feel like a chicken in a fox house, looking out at all you bright, attentive people, who rumor has it, are so gracious to local law enforcement." That got him the laugh he wanted. "But, I want all of you to know, that I do accept you're all probably smarter than I am. Doesn't matter to me. I'm here to help, not get credit."

"Secondly, the ten cases we turned up, were discovered in an I.T. search of only four hours. These cases are each, among the most horrible murders I've seen in my 24 years in law enforcement. That's why we didn't want you seeing the photos. We have two assignments. Find out how many more of these are out there. And, using these murder pictures, crime scene evidence, your sophisticated computer systems, and old fashioned investigating, find out just who this person is, and stop him. Stop him now."

Tom nodded to a man at the laptop and the first slide appeared. It was the cover of the file with a title added. It said:

Tracker

"Special Agent Tillman asked me to come up with a name for this investigation. This word, best describes what we're trying to do...find him. It also applies to him. He is a man hunter. He stalks his prey, and kills them in hideous fashion. Next slide, please."

The next slide showed different variations of the composite sketch that had been drawn. It showed several ideas of what the suspect might look like. With and without cap, glasses, bald, bearded, etc. But, it was pretty vanilla, white male, 25-35, yada, yada, yada.

"In each of these cases, you are going to be shocked and sickened by this man. But remember this, he is an expert hunter. He is an expert killer. No one who this man had tried to kill, has survived. And most of the killings were double homicides. Yes, ten murder scenes, eighteen victims. I understand that Special Agent Tillman, would like to say a few more words, now."

Tom stepped back to his chair, as Tillman retook the lectern. "For those of you wondering about the others on the dais, Assistant SAC Lyle Gordon will lead the

'Tracker' task force. Agent Davis-Leigh in second command. You all know our resident profiler, Dr. Singh, I brought him this folder last night, and asked him to say a few words about the killer. Dr. Singh, if you will be so kind."

The man who was second-generation American walked slowly to the podium. He was a smallish, thin man, wearing a light linen suit. He spoke perfect English, with only the hint of an accent.

"I don't know enough to be in the position to enlighten you about this despicable human being. Just these photographs, show me he is a man who likes to punish.

He would rather kill slowly and painfully. Yes, he fits the general stereotype of the serial murder criminal. Other than that, I would propose that we cannot, at this point understand him. Was he sexually or otherwise abused as a child? Is he impotent? Does he speak to his dog, like David Berkowitz?"

"The one thing I believe so far, is that he has no motive against his victims. He is a random killer. A sociopath who chooses his prey. I doubt that even he knows why he chose them. A person who carries no motive, is the hardest to catch."

The doctor retook his seat. Tillman made an announcement, "You people here will be assigned to different aspects of the task force. We have four personnel from I.T. They will divide the country into segments and search for additional all the crimes which might fit our unsub. We have two from forensics, who will go the known crime scenes for follow-up, I've assigned four, agent teams to go to each known and future murder scenes, and six agents, plus Gordon and Davis-Leigh assigned to run the investigation from conference room 3-C, for the duration. Now, you can all review your folders.

The meeting broke up, and Tom pulled SAC Tillman aside. "There's something else I just found out." Tillman smiled, "All communications from this building are monitored in real time. I know about the ear. You were smart not to bring it up until we can establish it's relevance."

A scream came from the center of the room. The photos were like nothing the I.T. agent had ever seen. She put her head in her hands, but could not hold back the tears as they flowed down her cheeks.

Tom and the SAC looked at the agents assembled there. Their looks were those of horror and revulsion. A couple ran from the conference seeking the nearest bath room.

"This one's going to be tough," Tillman whispered. "But, even sweeter when we catch the bastard," Tom retorted.

Tillman smiled. I knew he was right for the job, he thought.

Twenty Four

At the subsequent meeting, Assistant SAC Gordon called for quiet and reviewed his notes. He was a tall man, late thirties, medium build. There was a serious tone to his voice, and Tom had been told by the SAC that Gordon didn't suffer fools lightly.

"I've spoken to Agent Davis-Leigh, about organizing the task force. We've decided that we would focus on the known crimes, for the first few days. It's a good idea to try to get into this guy's head, his habits, his wherewithal, using the existing crimes, and while we have the services of our SAPD friend, who knows the cases better than anyone.

After two or three days, we anticipate that I.T. will come up with more data which will require follow-up. If Detective Granger and I decide it is a probable match, we will give it to the agent in charge of that section of the country. If you look behind your chairs, you will see six white boards which divide the country into the same number of areas. Northeast, southeast, northern mid-west, southern mid-west, northwest, and southwest. The contiguous 48 states, only. The crimes we've attributed to the stalker, are all in the southeast, and southern mid-west.

We'll begin with the crimes we are most familiar with, and start there, as a team. Then break off when your part of the country gets a hit. Gordon looked up, almost apologetically. "I not hoping more crimes will be uncovered. But we've got to be prepared." He handed out assignment sheets to each of the six agents. On each one was printed their section:

McNally - northeast
Colby - southeast
Tomkins – upper mid-west
Jenkins – lower mid-west
Blair – northwest
Perez - southwest

"I know this looks gerrymandered, but I tried to keep population in mind, and not square miles or number of states per agent. Any comments?" No agent raised any objection. Tom did. "Yes detective," Gordon said to Tom, who held up his hand.

He rose from his chair and pointed to the map. "Since Moss Point and Slidell are the two incidents we know more about, and are the most recent murders, I suggest you put Slidell in the southeast, so we can work those cases side–by–side. They're less than 90 miles apart, it might help us get a quicker start."

Gordon looked around the table, sensing the general agreement. Davis-Lee was nodding as well. "Makes sense to me, let's do it."

Tom remained standing. "One more thing I found out only minutes from this morning's meeting. We know that at least two of the victims, one each from Slidell and Morgan City, had their ear cut off. We'll need to follow up on that. It may be important. A trophy."

It was the first piece of evidence which definitively established a link between two crimes. The group of FBI agents started going over what was known of the crimes, one by one.

Tom's job was to learn more details about the crimes, especially the "ear" connection. He started calling the local law enforcement officials. He had really only spoken in depth to the sheriff in Moss Point, and the chief in Slidell.

I.T. started mining from the internet using key words, through various search engines, including the NCIC.

Forensic agents were having autopsies and post mortems faxed or emailed from the 9 localities. They received tox screens, blood tests, stomach contents, and anything else which might lead them to the killer.

Finally, the group decided to take a break for a late lunch. It was already 1:30. and Assistant SAC Gordon, felt like a great deal of planning and groundwork had been laid. Now they had to get to the basics of this criminal investigation, which really hadn't changed over the last hundred or so years. Interrogation, scene analysis, victimology, and other evidence would break the case.

Most of the group ate together in a nice lunchroom, built by the taxpayers. The food was not inexpensive, but it wasn't free, either.

Gordon grabbed two chicken salad wraps, two diet Cokes, and took the elevator to the 4th floor. Hoping to have lunch with SAC Tillman.

Bill Tillman was in his office trying to break through the brick wall created by the CIA on the only hard evidence they had, the prints found under the dryer at the Rosette home. Gordon knocked on the door, stuck his head in, and Tillman waved him in. Gordon put a bag containing 1 wrap, and a diet Coke on Tillman's desk.

Tillman covered the phone, "I've been on hold for the director, for over ten minutes now. I'm stuck, I can't hang up, I'll just have to wait."

In just a couple of minutes a pleasant voice came on the phone and said the director was getting off a conference call and would speak to Tillman in about a minute.

Finally, he was connected. After a few pleasantries, he told the Director of the FBI the obstacles put up by the CIA. Of course the director had already been briefed. Robert Townsend was no one's fool. He'd kept his position for over fourteen years now, and knew how the game was played inside the beltway.

Townsend told the SAC that he had just been on a conference call with the DOJ and CIA heads. Their conclusion was that no one would be allowed access to this file, until evidence was produced which proved linkage between the cases. The director was told by the CIA that the coding on the envelope meant that the file inside was one of an "asset," which should be protected. In other words, come back to us if, and only if, you had a lot more hard connections between the murders.

Tillman knew that the word "asset," was code for assassin, or spy at best. He didn't know about the "ear" connection, because Gordon hadn't had time to tell him yet. He thanked the director, and the phone in D.C. was cut off.

Gordon had heard the conversation from Tillman's end, only. He informed him of the missing ear in two cases, and suggested they call the director back.

"No," Tillman said, leaning back in his chair. "When we go back, I want to go back loaded with connections. Doing things in "dribs & and drabs," will only get me transferred to a station in Anchorage." He looked up, "And remember Lyle, shit rolls downhill. Tell the techies to add 'missing ear' to the key words, and see if we get another hit."

The director was clear, if this killer stays close to us, it's our case. If it branches out of Texas into California, or up north, it'll be run nationally. We may be on the team, even the lead team, but we won't have final control.

Twenty Five

Travis Bayne was walking west along highway 90. It was like old home week. He was keenly familiar with this part of the country. He had just passed the turn off for Raceland, when he heard a man moaning for help. He couldn't locate the source, until he heard it again.

Because the bayou country was so low roads had been built on fill ground, with gravel, oyster shells, and so forth, before being paved. The effect was that the major roadways had no shoulder, and a fall-off of six feet or so. Travis stopped, and craned his neck over the road, looking toward the cries for help.

There was a half-dressed man, entangled with a motorcycle, a Harley Davidson Travis though. A big bike, and the driver was pinned under it. The man looked to be broken up pretty badly. There was no telling how long he had been here. You couldn't see him from the road, and no one would have heard him over the noise of their own vehicle.

Travis scuttled down the embankment, just before one of the many short bridges in the area. He walked over to where Leland Bergeron lay. He could see that both legs were broken, with bones exposed to the air, thick with flies feeding on the wounds and the pools of blood which had run down the bank. His head and spine were tilted at an odd angle. Travis knew from his battlefield experience that the man would be dead any minute.

"Get me to the hospital in Houma, Boudreaux begged. I'll pay you, that's my home. Bring me to the hospital, and I'll give you ten thousand dollars."

Bayne checked his pockets, his sport coat was snared in the spokes of the rear wheel. Travis found the man's wallet and cell phone. It said Leland Bergeron lived at 1802 Lafayette St., in Houma. As for the cell phone, there was no signal out here. There was about $80 in cash, Travis took that.

The motorcycle helmet was very blackened, and had "Ragin' Cajun" on it in script. It hung from one of the back "saddle bags" still on the Harley. The driver hadn't used it. He wiped down the phone and wallet and returned them to the man's pockets.

"How did this happen?" Travis asked, trying to get more information. "Shacked up with a married woman," husband came back. I was lucky to get out of there." Maybe, maybe not, Travis thought.

"You have anyone to notify in Houma?" Travis asked. "I've got a cousin across town, and the rest of my family is in Bayou Cane, on the north side. I live alone. I'm in the oil business," he said just before the death rattle of his last breath.

Travis had all the information he needed.

Lester whispered, "*I want an ear.*" Travis, reached down with the KA-BAR, and sliced off the ear. The man was committing adultery, and should have worn the helmet. He'd never miss the ear.

Travis filled the saddlebags with rocks, and rolled the wrecked Harley and Leland into a bayou about 50 feet away. He watched them sink into the swamp. The crawfish and gators would be well fed, tonight. Now on to Houma. A small detour. But possibly a prosperous one, as well. Travis walked on the left side of the road all the way to Houma. It was small, Louisiana highway #182. The first sign he came to said "Houma...6m." He would get there just before sundown, if he was correct.

Travis stopped at a small, locally owned gas station just inside the city limits. It was festooned with a Confederate flag, and several "New Orleans Saints" posters. The best ones had the old "Who Dat" slogan. He asked the old codger behind the desk if there was a city map available. The man pointed to an old map pinned to the wall next to a pay phone. Much hadn't changed around here in the past 50 years, Travis surmised.

He walked over, and almost immediately say Lafayette St. It looked like it was less than a mile away. He memorized the cross streets and turns, thanked the attendant, and left. Taking his path, he found the home in question. He walked by to do an early recon. He didn't hear a sound.

There was a "Motel 6" across the street. He decided to get a room, maybe for the night, and watch the house for a while.

A heavy set "mulatto" girl sat behind the counter. She was probably sixteen or seventeen. He flashed his bright smile, she smiled back, sheepishly, and took $30 in cash for the room. She didn't ask him to sign the register.

Travis knew she would pocket the money, and not tell her boss about the new man in room B-7. "Anything else you be wantin'?" She hinted. "My name's Tina."

Travis leaned forward on the counter. "I've got to visit an old friend tonight, but if things work out, I'll be back next week. You'll still be here?" The girl nodded anxiously. "I'll be staying here again, if I'm lucky."

Travis watched out the motel room window for an hour or so. It was on the second floor, and offered a clear view of the house, and it's surroundings. There was no activity. There were no nearby neighbors, the lots were good-sized. He hadn't seen or heard any children or, heaven forbid, dogs.

At about 9:30, he slipped out of his room, walked down the outside walkway away from the office so the girl wouldn't see him if she looked. He had a black windbreaker, over his shirt.

He carried the silenced Glock inside the waistband of his jeans. The sheath with the KA-BAR, was in his jacket. Leather gloves were stuffed in his rear jeans pocket. He walked a few houses past the subject home, then crossed the street. He walked like he had no place to go, at least not in a hurry.

He turned the corner of Lafayette and Honduras Streets, and slipped behind the corner home. Leland's house was the second one on the street. He moved like a summer breeze, and stayed still in the shadow cast by the back door. He waited for dogs, or motion detector lights, and there were none. The lock was a 60-second pick job. Once inside the home he started searching the usual places where people hid cash. With his penlight he looked in the closet, and on the top shelves. There was a nice Remington 30-30, but those could be traced, and he had all the weapons he'd ever need. Travis pulled a dining room chair into the hall way and pushed up on the panel which covered the scuttle access to the attic. He pulled his way up and examined the attic, nothing.

He looked under the bed and between the mattress and box springs, without finding a thing. He tore through the bureau drawers, even feeling for things taped to the underside of them or the nightstand. He sat in the middle of Boudreaux's bedroom and thought.

The garage. Inside the garage was a fairly new "Honda Accord," a few tools, a place where the Harley usually sat, and a freezer. A freezer, he thought, with a lock on it. He jimmied it open with a pry bar from the red tool box. Lots of meat, looked like venison. He examined the packets and found nothing inside which wasn't edible.

Travis had read about the Louisiana congressman who was found with lots of money in his freezer. He figured that changed the hiding place for many citizens.

I should have got his hiding place from him while he was alive, Travis told himself. Well, too late for that now. He went to the kitchen, searched the freezer and refrigerator...nada.

The always suspicious cookie jar was empty. Now he opened the panty, and started with the sugar and flour containers. They were the largest. Nothing but flour and sugar inside.

Then the usual things. "Uncle Ben's" rice, a spice rack, "Wesson Oil," two boxes of "Count Chocula" breakfast cereal, a dozen cans of soup. Travis stopped. "Count Chocula?" Boudreaux had no children. This was kid's food. Definitely out of place.

Travis reached to the top shelf, and knew he'd found the stash. The boxes were heavy, much too heavy for cereal. Inside was the cash. There were several bundles of cash He dumped them on the kitchen table. Looking around the kitchen, Bane spotted an old brown grocery bag. It was from "Winn Dixie." Travis put the cash in the bag, rolled the top of the bag so no one could see inside, and began his departure.

He didn't try to clean up. He had ransacked the house. It would have taken hours to get everything back in place. Besides, he had worn his gloves the entire time he was there.

Travis turned the door knob so it would lock behind him when he left. He stayed in the shadow for 5 minutes, again. He traversed the neighbor's back yard in seconds, and walked casually down the street with his grocery bag under his arm.

On the way, he passed a "Burger King." What the heck, he thought, I'm hungry. He went in, ordered a double whopper with cheese, fries, and a medium coke. He still had his Saints hat and sunglasses on. No one could recognize him. He paid, got his change and returned to the Motel 6, the long way, avoiding the office. He ate greedily. It was the best meal he'd had in a few days. For all the walking he did, Travis could afford the extra carbs.

He had used discipline regarding the money. Now he was ready to count it. The total was $22,440, mostly in twenties. He put the money back in the brown sack, and placed it inside the backpack he wore, sliding it under the bed. Travis was excited. It had been a great day.

Just then, there was a knock on his door. Shit, where did I screw up, he asked himself. He went to the door and saw the girl from the motel's office outside. Had she been following him? Did she see him at Boudreaux's house?

He put the knife away, under the nearest bed pillow. Travis opened the door with his best "good Travis" smile. "Hi, nice surprise, he said."

"Thought I'd take a chance you got back early," the girl said coyly. "Could I come in? I've got some nice weed."

"You tell anyone you were coming here?" She shook her head from side to side as Travis looked up and down the outside hallway. "No," she said, "And I've got a couple of days off coming, starting now." "What about the maid?" She slipped the "Do Not Disturb" sign over the outside of the door handle. "She sees this, no way she's coming in. Girl got fired couple of months ago, entering a room with the DND on the door. No way."

Travis waved her in. He was relieved. But what, if anything had she seen. Well, like she said, she took a chance. They both sat on the bed and she quickly slid her hand to the crotch of his jeans, feeling something rising to meet it. "How do you like it," she asked. "Straight up," he replied. "Lets smoke a 'J' first. That's when I does my best work," she smiled eagerly.

The joints were good, he had tried marijuana a couple of times during his mid-east deployment, but the sex was great. This girl knew what she was doing, four times. She even supplied the condoms. After each time, Travis flushed the condoms, "Don't want to leave a mess," he said.

The next morning, Travis policed the room. The wrappers and cup from Burger King went into the backpack. He pulled the linens from the bed, and folded them inside the windbreaker he would carry under his arm. He would dump them in a maid's hamper which would be on one of the floors, or in the trash bin on the way out. The bundle would look awkward, but it would only be for a minute.

Earlier, Tina had gone on her merry way, Travis had promised her two more nights of good sex and drugs, and paid her $60 for room the next two nights. He warned her to keep her mouth shut, and come back after dark. "Don't worry," she said, "I need this job, ain't many out there these days."

Travis took a shower and shaved, both activities done while wearing the shower cap provided by the hotel. He knew they could get DNA from hair follicles he might leave in the shower drain. Beard shavings would go straight down the sink drain. He left the hot water running in the sink for several extra minutes.

After getting dressed and set to depart, he looked up and down the hall, then downstairs over the rail. The laundry cart was conveniently there, already half filled with linens. His deposit wouldn't be noticed.

He slipped out of the room, the DND sign still hanging

outside the room. Travis started walking, down the steps, along the first floor hallway, and quickly dumped the linens in between the pile of soiled sheets already there.

He turned to walk down the street. State highway #182 was only three blocks away. Suddenly, out of nowhere, two State Police cruisers, and a Houma police squad car screamed past him. The all came to a screeching halt in front of the house owned by Leland Bergeron. What was this about, Travis wondered.

Obviously the body had been found. But by who? And how so quickly?

About the same time, two sheriff's cruisers pulled into the yard of Marty Saucier. It seems Ms. Hebert had called the Sheriff of Terrebonne Parish, after witnessing the end of the fight and Leland Bergeron's messy getaway.

The high beams and rollers illuminated the yard. An officer crouched behind his car's door and yelled into a bullhorn, "Marty Saucier, this is the Sheriff's Department. Come out of the house with your hands on your head."

Marty peeked out the window. He figured he Leland had filed a battery charge against him. A charge which would never stick under the circumstances. He complied with the order, and walked out the front door barefoot, wearing only a "wife-beater" t-shirt, and a pair of jeans.

The sheriff's men kept him covered with their handguns and even a Mossberg pump, until he was handcuffed behind his back, his chest on the hood of the cruiser. Marty was facing across the street, where he saw Ms. Hebert was under her porch light, flipping him off again.

What came next shocked him. "Martin Saucier, you are under arrest for the murder of Leland Bergeron. You have the right to remain silent, you have the right to an attorney," Marty blurted out, "I don't need no attorney, I got..." "Let me finish boy, then you can tell your side of the story."

After Marty was properly read his Miranda rights, the cops pushed him in the back seat, and scratched out of the oyster shell driveway, taking Marty to the Houma lockup. A female and a male sheriff stayed behind to question Bernadette Saucier.

Bernadette was shaking, "Leland's dead?"

"Looks like he crashed his Harley into some rocks near the bayou on highway #182. A local, with his son, was poling a pirogue, looking for gators, turtles, whatever, and the bike scratched the bottom of his boat. It's only about two feet deep there, so the fisherman got out to see what was up. He called in a motorcycle accident. Said he ran through this stretch of bayou, twice everyday, the wreckage wasn't there this morning."

"Thing is, we thought it was just an accident too. But, the body was all mangled, Ms. Hebert had called the altercation into the sheriff, and the body was weighted down, like nobody wanted it found. We put 2 and 2 together, and came out here."

Bernadette started crying, "They had them a fight, it was bad, but Marty didn't kill him. He was here with me, ever since Leland drove off."

"You'd swear to that in a court of law?" the female

sheriff asked. "With my hand on the 'good book', and as God is my witness, I would."

The deputies looked at each other. "She needs to be here when her girls get home, anyway. She ain't going nowhere. We'll see what Marty says, and go from there."

In Houma, Marty was telling the authorities the exact same story. He didn't deny "puttin' a whippin' on Leland," after catching him shacked up with Bernadette. But he was adamant that he didn't leave the house since Leland made his getaway.

"Ask my wife. Hell, ask old lady Hebert. Ain't nothing going on she don't know about."

"Don't worry," said the lead interrogator, "we will."

For the next three hours, while the police and sheriff were sorting things out, Travis had walked the one mile up state road #24, and started walking on highway 90 again, toward Amelia.

By the time Marty Saucier was released, Travis was in the back of a pick up truck in St. Mary's Parish, almost to Morgan City. He didn't want to stop there. He'd been there on a mission before. Luckily the driver was going all the way to New Iberia. Travis figured he'd jump off and spend the night at a cheap hotel there.

Twenty Six

By the end of the second day, the task force had twenty three cases to review from around the country. The great majority, sixteen, seemed to be in the coastal states, plus Georgia. They would send field teams out to investigate only after the task force had a 90% certainty that it was linked to Tracker. The group discussed how they should prioritize them. As strong as their resources were, they were still limited to one agent per area of the U.S.

Gordon, the ASAC was arranging to have staffers work through the night using a set of priority protocols to rank the top cases. He thought a fresh set of eyes was needed. No one was a veteran of this case, not even Tom, but having outsiders rate the probabilities would help them all see things in a fresh perspective.

There was a lot of discussion on what clues and signs were significant. Angela Davis-Leigh thought that chronology should be the 1st priority, as they would include the most recent crimes, then couples would be weighed, then the relative savagery of the killings. Tom disagreed. Tom thought that "missing ear" was a trademark which would validate a murder. Because a case did not include that reference did not eliminate it from consideration, but having that reference seemed too important to be coincidental.

The group finally decided to set up one large white board, and investigate by similarities. Per Tom's recommendation they would be (1) ear, (2) brutality, (3)rural location.

The group would reconvene at 8 a.m. tomorrow morning. Tom was anxious to see what the staffers, who were all FBI agents, deduced from the mountain of case files in the room. After sorting, the chart should began to reveal a more disciplined view into the atrocities.

Crime scene photos were emotional. White boards and graphs, much less so.

This was the starting point. This was where all the factual evidence, not theory or conjecture, was sorted into a single format. The group left the conference room, dissolving into the night, with the staffers taking over.

Tom called Toni and gave her an update. Tomorrow could be a breakthrough day or another mess of confusion and disappointment. The good, and probably the bad thing was, the results were out of his control. Fresh people were on the case who would develop the consistencies in the cases, if he was right.

Tom had arranged to have a late dinner with Rosa, but it wouldn't be that late. He called her on his cell while driving to her place. It was only 6:45, but it seemed that he had been cooped up for days, and needed someone to talk to, if only to hear himself think. He drove into Rosa's driveway , and sat for 5 minutes before ringing the bell.

"I just feel this guy out there," he confessed to Rosa. "I'm not going crazy, I just think there's planning and a huge connection to the crimes, right in front of us."

Rosa listened, but there wasn't much to say. Tom played with his carne asada dinner, but couldn't eat. He was wired like Rosa had never seen him.

He looked up and found a weak smile for the woman he was in love with. "It's not the food...it's great, you know..." Rosa smiled back and said, "I know Tom, I know."

Tom left to struggle with a sleepless night, again. He tossed and turned through the fitful night. He took a walk outside at 2 am, tried watching Australian football on one of ESPN's sub-channels, and eventually showered, dressed, and had coffee at 6. was there at 7:45. An agent was posted outside the conference room. Tom tried to brush past him, and the agent shook his head. "No one in until 8, detective. You can wait over there with them," he said nodding to a group of several other agents on the task force. There were 5 others who couldn't sleep either, including Davis-Leigh. They had beaten him in for a quick look at the results as well. "Hi buddy," she said.

Tom laughed at himself, some detective, I was so focused I didn't even see them waiting, he thought to himself.

"I thought all you Feds were a heartless bunch of vampires," Tom kidded. And now you're trying to tell me you all care about this as much as I do."

Another young agent retorted, "And we all thought you were a clueless old man, until yesterday. Seems like you just can't trust good old solid prejudices any more."

They made small talk until 7:58, when Gordon showed up. "SAC Tillman isn't in yet, so I'm in charge. Agent please let your 'drifters' in to see the show.

And, what a show it was. They all sat back and saw the chart. It was something to behold.

	Missing	Discovery	Name &	City	Cause of			
Case#	Ear	Date	#Persons	State	Death	Children	Dogs	Setting
Tracker Case Evaluation								
1	Y	1/11/2011	Rosette, 2	Slidell, La.	Multiple	No	No	Rural
2	Y	1/19/2010	Forcet, 2	Morg.City, La.	Multiple	No	No	Rural
3	Y	2/18/2009	Perez, 2	Stowell, Tx.	Multiple	No	No	Rural
4	Y	11/18/2009	Neal, 2	Fairhope, Al.	Ax	No	No	Farm
5	?	10/12/2009	Odom, 2	Grand Bay, Al.	Explosion	No	No	Farm
6	?	10/18/2010	Bray, 1	Quincy, Fl.	Beheaded	No	No	Dairy
7	?	12/13/2010	Bunch, 1	Moss Pt. Ms.	Explosion	N/A	N/A	Road
8	?	12/19/2010	Tate, 2	Moss Pt. Ms.	Multiple	No	No	Farm
9	?	10/25/2010	Branson, 2	Dufuniak, Fl.	Crucified	No	No	Farm
10	?	2/17/2010	Cummings, 2	Gonzales, Tx	Hung	No	No	Ranch

The chart was stunning in it's clarity There was no reason to believe that these crimes were not committed by the same man. The first four were identical in their components. After that, the clues were blurred by decomposition, animal feedings, and in one case decapitation. This was linkage in several different areas of criminal behavior. No one could dispute that.

After hours of debate in the early stages of the investigation, the "board" brought these crimes into a crystal clear focus.

In about 5 minutes, Tillman walked in. He could feel the excitement in the room. He looked at the chart with the others, nodding his head.

Almost immediately, another agent came into the room with a note for the SAC. Tillman unfolded the paper. "It's from I.T. A murder yesterday in Houma, Louisiana. Perp tried to make it look like an accident. Victim's house was ransacked. The dead man was missing his left ear.

He looked at Gordon, who pointed to the evidence board with a shrug. Tillman stood up from his chair and announced, "I'm calling the director. Have a copy of this chart, with Houma added to it, emailed to the director before I get him on the phone. You've got 20 minutes."

Then he paused as he was walking out the door, "Great work gang, now get back on it and make me look credible. I'm going out on a limb, and remember..." half the room recited a phrase they were obviously familiar with, "shit rolls downhill. "

"And listen, people, we're still not public here. Nothing out of this building without my prior permission."

Davis-Leigh interrupted, "Boss, at least, let us get the sketches out, with a reward and a phone number. We don't have to say what it concerns, just say that he is wanted for 'questioning'. If we keep it low key, a friend or acquaintance might call in. With the different versions of the look, on display at post offices and law enforcement buildings, we could get lucky. We might even stop another killing."

Tillman agreed, "Good idea. Have the number linked to our office hot line. Gordon, double the staffing on the hotline, give them a clue of what we're doing, so they can weed out the dognappers and UFOs."

Twenty Seven

It was 10:25 in Langley, Virginia. The Attorney General of the United States, Sam Simons was being stonewalled by the Chief of the Central Intelligence Agency, David Markham. The agencies had been at each others throats for years. 9/11, made the pressure unbearable.

"Sam, you know we don't operate domestically." Technically it was illegal for the CIA to be involved with situations in this country. They were supposed to work outside the U.S. only. The 9/11 event had blurred those lines to some degree, but the law was still the law.

"Dammit, David, for the third time, I didn't say that. I said that you have information which we need in solving a domestic case, an I.D."

"Well, you're going to have to get more specific than this, I don't have a clue what you're talking about. After all. I may be a spook, but I'm not a mind reader."

The A.G. lowered his voice and calmed himself. "It's in the last two communiqués I sent directly to you. Is someone screening your mail, from me? That's the only way you wouldn't know what I was referring to. I'll say this one more time, sealed file #3826a41. I need this man's name and jacket."

The CIA chief responded coolly, smiling through the phone, "Why, might I ask?"

The Attorney General was a millisecond away from a cardiac event, when his counterpoint added, "I sent the request down to operations, yesterday. You'll have your answers today." Then, there was nothing but dial tone on the phone in the A.G.'s hand.

Two floors below, the deputy director of HUMINT (human intelligence) was holding a "come to Jesus" meeting with his number two and three people, Ron McShay and David Reynolds.

Deputy Director Michael Riordan sat shaking his head. "I told you there'd be blowback on this. I told you to handle it."

"We tried," McShay said feebly, "we tried twice."

"Annnnd, what happened?" Riordan asked. Reynolds admitted, "We got three ears back, in the mail. One of the packages was addressed to my home. **He knows where I live....**"

"So this guy, this guy...what's his name?" "Bayne," McShay said, "Travis Bane."

"So this Bayne's been out there for a couple of years, playing catch me if you can, and we can't. That about sum it up?"

"Yeah, boss," McShay admitted, "we can't."

Riordan sat back, and made a steeple with his fingers. "Idiots, he was a 'kite', cut the strings, but I want in on the apprehension. I'll give him up, but we want to show some remorse. He sustained PTSS, injured emotionally, yada, yada, yada."

Riordan smiled," Didn't you tell me once, you remember when you were bragging about this new operative you found, that he an orphan? We've got all kind of ways to deal with this situation, you just have to choose the outcome which would be best for the agency"

"But boss," McShay pleaded, "we can't operate here, in the U.S., and we sure as hell don't want him brought in for questioning and a trial. That could be embarrassing to a great many people. People even more powerful than us."

"Exactly, I'll cut the deal, he's one of our own boys, etc., etc. I want you idiots, to get in tight with the Bureau, and beat the FBI to him. Do I have to spell it out? You two be there tomorrow, for a briefing. Don't volunteer intel, but don't try to hide it either. Why are you still here?" The underlings fled the office, and Riordan relaxed for the first time today. He shook his head and smiled.

Bayne...what a waste of talent, he thought.

Riordan yelled to his secretary, "Call satellite tech, I want ears on FBI San Antonio, today! Landlines, emails, cell phones both in and outbound, all of it, in real time."

Twenty Eight

On a crisp Wednesday Tom left the FBI office, on schedule, at 5 o'clock, for the first time since he started his temporary assignment, ten days ago. He had been told that he would be needed another few days, hen returning to the SAPD homicide squad. He yearned to be among his fellow officers again, but he had learned quite a bit on his temporary duty, and in fact, had probably contributed more to the case than had been expected.

He felt vindicated in his initial assessment of the case. He had his doubters in the beginning, justifiably so, but in what would later be called the beginning of the end, his instincts had won out.

Tom drove the short distance home to his small 3-bedroom single story, just off Blanco road on the north side of San Antonio. It was a quiet, peaceful area, still mostly full of empty-nesters like him. However, in the past few years, young couples with children had started moving in around him. The schools were good, shopping close by, and home prices were affordable. It was one of the best, inexpensive places to live in San Antonio.

There was nothing wrong with this neighborhood cycle. Neighborhoods were born, developed, matured, and then one or two generations later, started turning younger again, with an influx of new families. Tom understood the transition, it was just a little noisier every month or so, like it had been when he first moved here decades ago. and he had loved the area ever since.

Lately, he had started thinking about the forty acres he now owned outside a small town named Boerne (Burny), about twenty five miles north of the city. It was close in proximity, but was entirely different from the hustle and bustle of San Antonio in so many ways.

He had come into a small inheritance about four years ago, when his stepfather died. It was less than $20,000, and when he thought of what to do with the unexpected windfall, he decided to invest in a quiet future. After a great deal of research aided by his own knowledge of the area, he found an estate for sale.

It was a medium-sized property simply known as the old "Breeden Ranch". The Breeden family had owned the land since Texas became a state in 1845. The land came with a small 3-bedroom house, which Tom would have to expand, or tear down and build new. Ms. Breeden, now 88 years young, had come to the point in her life where it was necessary for her to have around-the-clock, assisted care.

Also, her deteriorating health situation meant she had to be somewhere close to modern medical facilities, and that entailed moving to San Antonio. Tom wanted to go in the opposite direction. Not wanting to be viewed as a predator by his soon-to-be neighbors, Tom went to the Realty firm which was marketing the property. He met with the broker, a third generation Realtor named Billy Ray Watkins.

Billy Ray was in his early forties, casual in attire, true Texas in his speech, and a consummate professional in his business. Tom asked simply, "I know real estate is priced to allow room for negotiation, maintenance, marketing expenses, and other unanticipated items. So Mr. Watkins, what I want from you is what's the Breeden property worth, as-is, an all cash transaction, today? I'm not a negotiator. Watkins thought about the question, and decided Tom was on the square. Some people asked for your best price, then tried to negotiate their way down from there. Billy Ray didn't put Tom in that category.

Mr. Granger, I'm not authorized to offer you an answer on anything but the listed price, which is $27,500. It's just not my decision. That decision belongs to the seller. But if you offered $22,000, as-is, and as you indicated, a cash closing within 30 days, I'd be inclined to support that offer and ask that it be accepted.

Tom replied, smiling as he did when he thought he was being treated fairly, "Write it up and I'll sign it. I'll also leave you a check for ten thousand dollars, as a deposit of good faith, 'earnest money', I think you call it." Watkins pulled an envelope out of his desk titled, "Breeden", when Tom interrupted him. "But Mr. Watkins, there's always some greedy member of the family who thinks they can get a thousand dollars more. My offer is solid. It's $22,000, not $22,001. I make an offer, I'm done."

Don't worry, Mr. Granger, Emily Breeden is as smart as a whip. No one has her power-of–attorney. She's the only one who has to sign, it's not the family's decision.

Tom had asked Rosa to marry him, a few weeks ago. She had given him an enthusiastic yes, with the caveat that they would have to get Maria's and Anna's permission. He approached them, just as if he were asking for her hand from Rosa's deceased father.

There wasn't a moment of hesitation, they were very excited about the prospect. The girls had not known much of their birth father, KIA in the mid-east war. But they were proud of his sacrifice. They knew he was a patriot, dying so that others might be able to enjoy freedom.

They had gotten to know Tom in the past couple of years, and had adopted him, not the other way around. So the four of them would be a family soon. Tom wanted a perfect place for his family to live. Somewhere he didn't have to worry about the drugs, the gangs, and the drive-by shootings

Plus the public school system was spotty, even where Tom lived. Tom and Rosa didn't have the disposable income to continue private schools for the girls indefinitely, and lacked the time and talent required for home-schooling. The Boerne Independent School District seemingly offered better education. It was more diverse, due to the large number of transplanted Germans who had relocated almost two hundred years ago, and the class sizes were much smaller.

Tom loved the land around Boerne. Geographically, it was the beginning of the Texas hill country. Large stands of cottonwood, live oak, some natural cool spring water, and various rock formations, dotted the property. The fauna was abundant, deer, turkey, pheasant, with great bass fishing. Someday, soon, he would either expand or tear down and rebuild the old ranch house, modernizing it and making it large enough for a family of four.

Even though Interstate 10 ran through the small town, once you were less than a mile from the superhighway, you could imagine yourself in 19th century Texas. The pace was slow, the people honest, no one bothered to lock their doors at night. Tom felt comfortable in this rural setting. It was Texas. Here everybody knew everybody. On Tom's few visits to check on his property he had always gone out of his way to meet, and stay acquainted, with his future neighbors.

That was accomplished by coming to town on Sundays, attending church services, and then paying a visit to the general store on highway #46, afterward. The locals here were friendly, but you had to earn their trust.

Tom knew this, and also knew he'd have no problem. There was nothing fake about the town or himself. Once they discovered that their new landowner carried a badge, he was given extra special treatment.

In Boerne, they still respected the law, and the people who enforced it.

This Sunday, Tom had brought Rosa and her two girls with him. Rosa was a unsure of how a Hispanic would be viewed in this rural outskirt. After all, the newspapers had accounts of murders, drugs, and worse, on their headlines everyday. A fair share of those villains (and victims) were Hispanic, being citizens or illegal.

To her pleasant surprise, she was accepted immediately, and her daughters had the locals fawning on them from the beginning. Tom was no fool, he knew people.

There was a church picnic that afternoon. Tom had the foresight to previously accept the invitation for all four of them. Rosa had made a mild version of cabrito (young goat) with all the trimmings. It was a hit.

Then, the word got around that Rosa was a San Antonio cop, as well, and she was an overnight hero. The group in town felt that having police as neighbors, made the community a little more stable, and a lot more safe.

After too much food, tea, and dessert, the four newcomers made their goodbyes, promising to return soon. Five minutes later, on the drive home, Tom asked Rosa what she thought about Boerne, and more importantly, the people who lived there.

"I feel that people accept me...no, that's not right, they really want me, for the first time in a while. People in big cities, like San Antonio, look down on the police. Here, we're appreciated. The mood was such that I felt like I was asked to become a part of the community. I was as comfortable today, as I had been when I was a small girl, at my Abuela's (Grandmother's) casa, it was like I was at home."

"Girls?" Tom queried. There was a torrent of conversation, some English, some Spanish, all positive. Lots of talk about the food, the higher terrain, the peaceful surroundings, etc.

"Well, then you won't be disappointed that your Mother and I own forty acres up here, and plan to build our new ranch on."

With that, their important issues came up.

"Can we have a pony?" Maria bust forth. "At least a couple of dogs," Anna pleaded. Tom smilingly shook his head, ever the diplomat. "This is up to your Mother, you girls know that by now.

Rosa was grinning, with a well rehearsed answer, "I've always loved animals, but we'll talk about what type, and how many, when we get closer to a move-in date." Maria and Anna exchanged a big "high five." The answers seemed to satisfy them for now, especially Rosa's usage of the phrase "how many", left them encouraged.

The remainder of the half hour drive home to Rosa's was full of questions from the girls. "Can we have our own room? Will it be a one or two story?" and many more. Tom fielded these with a promise, "You two will help with the design, I promise." How much better could it get?

Tom was in heaven. For the first time in years, he was at peace with himself. The construction plans for the ranch had just moved forward to a priority position in his mind.

Book Four

Twenty Nine

Tom was dropping Rosa and her daughters off, when his cell phone buzzed him to attention. He recognized the prefix, it was from the FBI, specifically, SAC Tillman. On a Sunday, this must be big. He picked up, "Yes SAC Tillman (he was familiar with the drill, by now).

"I've told you to call me Bill the agent reminded him," but here it is, We've got ID on the Tracker, a woman who says she knows him, called the local FBI office, they called me, and here we are. We've also been honored with a CIA briefing at 3 p.m. tomorrow. How soon can you get here?" Tom looked at his watch, 3:15. Fifteen minutes, he answered. He was still dressed for church, jacket and all, so he looked his best. "Same conference room," Tillman bellowed, and hung up.

At 3:27, Tom pulled his pickup into the parking lot of the Federal complex. It was usually deserted on Sundays, but today, there were at least thirty vehicles parked there, and there were more coming. Tom entered the building, showing his temporary pass to the guards in the lobby, and hustling up the stairs toward the conference room on 3. Tom was intercepted by Tillman and Gordon on the way, and they waved him into Tillman's office closing the door behind them.

"This is a big break," Tillman said. Gordon elaborated. "We have someone who can ID the suspect, and pick him out of a lineup. Not only that, but we can use her as a litmus test against whatever our CIA friends offer us tomorrow. They sometimes speak the truth, but never the whole truth."

Gordon offered, "She's at the police station with the police chief of Hattiesburg, Mississippi, scared to death. Hattiesburg's a good sized town of about 50,000 people, partly due to hurricane Katrina, families relocating inland. It's about 45 miles to the Gulf. Their sole claim to fame was that their university (USM) was the only one to offer a football scholarship to a never before heard of high school quarterback named Brett Favre."

"The woman works for the Mississippi DMV, and saw the poster likenesses, luck, pure luck. I told their chief we'd call when you got in. you speak her lingo. I call in, 'FBI mam,' what do you think, she'd clam up. With you, we have a chance."

At 4:30, Granger dialed the number, identified himself, to the duty sergeant, and was transferred to the chief there. Tom explained that SAC Tillman was in the room along with Agents Davis-Leigh, and Gordon. Tom Granger. Chief Wiggins reciprocated. "I've got my deputy, city attorney Jim Sprague, and Delores Wilson from the city council, here on the speaker with me, along with Cindi Wheeler. And, we're recording."

"That's great," Tom commented. I'll do most of the talking, but the Special agent in Charge, Bill Tillman wants some things said on the record which will protect you. Is that good with you?" Chief Wiggins said, "Let the record say that she nodded."

Tillman began, "The thing I want to be clear and honest about to Ms. Wheeler is that this has nothing to do with her actions. We're not interested in what may or may not have happened before. We need help now. "

"I'm prepared to offer you a fifty thousand dollar reward, 100% FBI protection, and wash away any crimes you may have committed. And, that's being recorded, on both ends. Do you understand?" A meek voice came out of a cute pile of blonde hair... "What about my sister?"

"She has a sister," Chief Wiggins stated, "a twin sister, Tammy, I believe, she's in Corpus Christi." Tillman picked up the drift, "What I offered you, goes for her as well, money, protection, and complete exoneration. Are we understood?"

"All clear here," Wiggins answered, Cindi nodding beside him. "And, Ms. Wheeler nodded," the chief added.

"Good, time is critical," Tillman stressed, I'm turning this meeting over to Tom Granger. He knows more about what's been happening that the rest of us put together.

Thirty

Tom introduced himself, and asked Cindi to start at the beginning, goo slowly, and end where the twins had last seen Travis.

Cindi started slowly. "His name is Travis Bane. He saved the lives of my sister and me," was how she began to detail her horrible journey through the dominion of hell. Cindi was courageous in her testimony, She described the brutality against her and Tammy. She also told of the attempted emasculation and humiliation of Travis.

She seethed about the way Bob's wife, Gladys Monroe would always look the other way, almost every night as "Uncle Bob" had sex with them. How Gladys never tried to stop him. She told them about the boy who lived there before Travis came. A boy named Johnny, which she was sure Bob had caught and killed.

She talked about Travis coming up with a plan to escape. Cindi said that Travis could have escaped on dozens of occasions, but didn't want the twins to face the wrath of Bob. So Travis and Lester, his imaginary friend the girls had guessed, developed the escape plan.

Tom did what good cops do...let them talk, get it out of her system, Once the catharsis had run it's course, the healing could begin. An hour later, she finished with, "Tammy and I split ways about 5 years ago. She got married, neither of us can ever have children."

"If I had it to do over again, I'd do the same thing, I'd kill him and his evil wife again, and again, and again," she shouted as she finally broke down in tears.

Tom looked around the table. He and Davis-Leigh were both holding a box of Kleenex, Tillman had his sunglasses on, and Gordon had been holding his head in his hands for the last 20 minutes.

After a respectable time for everyone to collect them selves, Tom added, "You've been most courageous Cindi. I'm sure agent Tillman can have people in Corpus Christi keep an eye on your sister. Travis will never know we've talked, but you can never be too careful." He questioned, "When was the last time you or your sister heard from Mr. Bayne?"

Quickly, Cindi's mood changed. "You don't get it, do you? After all I've said, you still don't understand my feelings."

"Understand what?" Tom asked, in confusion.

"Travis Bayne is what. He saved our lives. Like the Bible says, he delivered us from evil. Without him, we'd have certainly died, but only after a few more years of hell on earth. Bob Monroe is the one who is responsible for Travis being like he is today. And now you people want to use our memories, our descriptions of him to hunt him down and kill him."

"And, to answer your question, that day in Carolina was the last we saw of Travis. That's the way he wanted it. He said that if we left with him, we'd always remember those horrible days at the Monroes' house. "The problem is I still remember those times, every night when I close my eyes. I still get only about four hours sleep. Sometimes when I wake up I'm afraid I'm back at the evil place.

Tillman interrupted. "Nothing cold be further from the truth young lady, and you can tell that to your sister too. I'm the head of the FBI taskforce, here. The FBI wants to bring him to justice, surely. But what is justice? From what you've told me, and I'm sure your sister would vouch for him, you're right, Travis was a victim."

"Travis saved your lives. And Travis needs professional help. I'm no doctor, but it would seem to me that the Monroes poisoned his mind and soul. They are to blame for much of this. We want to catch him...alive. We want the best medical minds available to evaluate him. We want him to be a positive part of society."

"Travis didn't just wake one morning and say 'I'm going to kill some people today', or 'The moon is full and has blood on it, so I've got to get some of it flowing'. His behavioral study could help him, and thousands of post-war vets around the country, live much more normal lives after professional therapy. Tillman offered, And the Bureau could help get you and your sister some of that therapy as well, at our expense."

"Believe me, this is not an Osama Bin Laden, 'dead or alive' capture we are about to undertake. However, if we can catch him before he does more harm, it will help his chances for a normal life."

Cindi nodded into the speaker. "I'll do all I can, to help Travis," she said.

Tom retook the interview. "I'm sorry, Ms. Wheeler, I'm just a local cop. I don't have the muscle like agent Tillman, to order protection for possible witnesses in other jurisdictions. If you'll give the name your sister is using now, and her address in Corpus Christi, Agent

Tillman will have her protection detail started right away." Cindi hesitated, "Mr. Granger, I'd appreciate you letting me tell Tammy know about this, first. I have to find out if she's ever told her husband. It wouldn't be right to surprise her family, she has a son as well.

Tom caught on. "She adopted?"

"Yes, he's three years old now. They named him Travis."

After a moment of disorientation, Tom pressed on. "There are just a few more questions which we need answered at this time. Some of them are harder, and if you don't want to answer, just say pass, and we'll move to the next one."

"Like I said, I'll do anything to help Travis."

"Cindi," said Tom, "here we go. The last time you saw Mr. Bayne was just outside Macedonia, North Carolina." Cindi answered in the affirmative.

"Did Bob Monroe ever molest Travis?" "No, definitely not. He would beat him, but I'm assuming you mean sexually, and the answer is no."

"Did Gladys Monroe...", "No, neither did she."

Tom took a deep breath and read from the scripted questions, "Did Travis Bayne ever molest you or your sister?" Cindi's eyes turned so cold that Tom could feel it through the phone lines. "No, he never hurt us, only helped us. Are you people stupid, or what? I've had it. This interview is over.

And Mr. Tillman, I want those promises you made me, including my sister, in writing, signed by someone with the authority to do so, in my hands quickly, or I'm going to the press, at least about my part of the story, until Tammy gives me her permission to share her experience with you."

Tom attempted to rescue the interview, "Ms. Wheeler, I apologize for he coldness and intrusive nature of these questions. Whoever wrote them was obviously some high priced head doctor. But if you don't mind, I have one question I always wondered about."

The phone line was silent, and Tom could see the two FBI agents raising their eyebrows and scrunching their shoulders.

Tom asked, "Did Mr. Monroe have a deformity of any kind, did he walk with a limp, or was blind in one eye, whatever?" "We know he was a painter, so it couldn't have been much."

Cindi had calmed down somewhat, and seemed to think it over. "No," she said, "besides being ugly and skinny, I guess he had all his pieces intact."

Tom slumped to the table. But Cindi, who couldn't see him, continued, "His sight was fine, and as long as you stood on the right side of him, he heard everything you said."

"What do you mean, what was the right side of him?"

Cindi finally got it, "His ear" she said, "He only had one good ear."

The FBI people stood up from their chairs in rapt attention to the speaker.

"Which one," Tom asked, trying to subdue his excitement.

"The right one," Cindi said, "he was born without a left, outer ear. He always tried to hide it, but it was obvious."

"Alright" Tillman said, "It's almost 5:00. I think we should let Ms. Wheeler contact her sister. We'll stay here and call back in an hour, that give you enough time?"

Cindi replied, "Yeah, she always has her cell with her, and she always answers it."

Thirty One

Cindi was been taken to a secure room in the Hattiesburg PD, along with a female officer posted outside the door, so that she could reach Tammy. She dialed her cell phone and he twin picked up on the second ring.

Cindi asked, "Are you at a place you can talk without being interrupted?"

"Sure, I'm at the mall, just me. Jimmy is babysitting Travis this afternoon...had to get away." her sister laughed. "Got some good news?"

"Yes, and no," she replied. "They are looking for Travis, not your Travis, our Travis."

Tammy turned pale, and sat on the ledge of the mall's center fountain as Cindi spilled her story. When she was finished with what she knew, and what she thought she knew, they were both in tears.

"No, I can't be involved. I've never told Jimmy about any of that goings on at the Monroes'. The doctor here said he probably had a low sperm count. I said no big deal, and we adopted. I told him I wanted to name the baby 'Travis', because it was an old family name, sort of like that guy at the Alamo had. Anyway, he'd never hurt us."

"Tammy, they want to help, they think he's sick from the war and all. These people know he needs treatments for the psychological disorder he has. They know he needs professional help, Cindi explained."

Tammy wasn't buying it. "They want to help him die, you mean. You're telling me that he's been all over the world on behalf of the government targeting people for death, and now he's in country killing innocent people, and they want to help him live? Do you actually think they would allow him to testify?"

"Cindi, I've got a good thing going here. My husband works hard and loves me, and little Travis is an angel. I can't see where my 'coming out of the closet' can be of any assistance to Travis Bayne."

"If they capture him alive, and he needs my help to avoid prison, or worse, I'll do anything I can to help. But until that happens, keep me out of it. I've got a lot to lose."

"Sister, I can't believe this, but I'm saying it anyway. We owe that man our lives. He could have deserted us many times, saving himself, but he didn't. And, now that he needs us, you turn your back. I hope you're sleeping better than I am."

Cindi folded her phone closed, and wept until her eyes were empty. The female officer gave her all the space she needed.

Then Cindi said aloud, "Maybe if I'd made something out of my life like my twin sister, I'd feel differently as well. But as for now, I'm going to do what's right for Travis Bayne."

The officer accompanied her back to the police chief's conference room, where everyone looked up from what they were doing, all eyes glued on Cindi Wheeler.

The chief announced, "Tom Granger just called in. He's on the speaker phone, is that OK with you? Cindi nodded her approval, and Tom was connected.

Officer Granger, your own the speaker the chief said. "Cindi, the ball is in your court."

"She won't help, at least not at this stage. She has a husband and baby to protect. She can't just come home one day and say, honey, did I ever tell you about the years I spent in North Carolina being sodomized and raped?"

"She did say that if Travis was caught and brought to trial. She'd corroborate my testimony, and try to help him as much as possible. But, until that happens, she doesn't want her name used in print, no police, no nothing."

"Travis doesn't know where she lives or even what her last name is. Only I have that. Most importantly, she doesn't think he would ever hurt her, or me. I agree with her."

"Cindi," Tom Granger asked, "we're going to be asking you a lot of questions, and you have to answer honestly just like in court. You're going to have to sign that it's the truth. It's called an affidavit."

"None of it will incriminate you, and I expect Agent

Tillman can have that paperwork you want which protects you and your sister, by tomorrow." Tillman was nodding.

"It would be a lot easier, and not as noticeable, if you were to come here. One new face in a city of two million, is a lot different than twelve different faces in a small town. You see where I'm headed?"

Cindi asked innocently, "Do you think I could get the time off, with pay, I mean, I've got bills?

Tillman interrupted, "I think Chief Wiggins and I could work that out, right, chief?"

"And maybe a few dollars spending money on the side," Wiggins laughed.

"Then Cindi, you go home and pack for 3 days," Tom said.

Davis-Leigh was working the Blackberry. Then she showed him the results. "There's a 12:40 flight out of Jackson, tomorrow, which arrives in San Antonio at 5:45. Do you think you can make that?"

"Sure" said Cindi, "It's only about 2 hours. I have to obey the speed limit, since I work for the DMV." That got some eyes rolling on both ends of the phone.

Tillman asked, "Chief Wiggins, could one of your officers escort Ms. Wheeler to the Jackson airport and down to San Antonio?"

Wiggins remarked, "I'm sure glad we don't have that

camera-phone thing here, because 10 hands just went up in the air, including mine. I think we can arrange that, if you'll authorize a stay over." "Done." Tillman exclaimed, "We have a deal." The chief said, "I'll fax you Ms. Wheeler's DMV photo I.D. so you'll know who to look for."

Tom said "Great, I'll pick you both up. I'll have a western hat on, but so will everyone else. I'll be at the exit carrying a card which says, 'Toni' on it. We'll find each other."

The trip the next day was uneventful, both driving to Jackson, and the Southwest flight. Cindi liked Southwest. She had only flown twice before, but Southwest employees seemed much more positive than most. It was like they enjoyed helping their passengers. What a concept, Cindi thought to herself.

Her companion, he said to call him Bobby, was dressed in plainclothes, so as not to stand out in a uniform.

Bobby knew the drill, and went directly to the TSA supervisor to offer his credentials, and disclose that he had a weapon. The supervisor walked them through security to their gate, and had a discussion with the ticket agent. Cindi and Bobby were the first to board.

At a little before 6 pm The crowd from Southwest Airlines began leaving the secured area of the terminal. Southwest had a well-deserved reputation for punctuality. Holding his sign, they soon spotted Tom, Cindi and the plainclothes Hattiesburg cop made their way over to him.

Cindi was a sight to behold. About 5'9", 130 pounds,

blond, blue eyed, early thirties, and as scared as a rabbit. The Mississippi officer introduced himself as Bobby Arnold. He was about 6'5" of Mississippi beef, on two legs. He had obviously won the lottery, being selected to escort Cindi.

"How'd you get picked for this assignment?" Tom asked. "You must be good at it. Maybe you did some protection work in the past?"

"Chief Wiggins is my uncle, he grinned." Tom laughed and said, "You're at the Airport Hilton, and here are the keys to a department Crown Vic. Try not to wreck it, it's my duty vehicle.

It's dark blue, unmarked of course. I assume you're carrying, but there's a 9mm Sig in a holster under the driver's seat. It's locked and loaded. I'm taking Cindi to a 'safe house', then I'll come back and meet you in the hotel lobby at 7:15.

We'll go to dinner on the feds. You did us a favor, we owe you that, at least. Here's my cell phone number in case you need it. The room is in my name, billed to the SAPD. Unfortunately, Cindi won't be joining us for dinner"

As instructed, Cindi carried on her small suitcase. No reason to spend time out in the open any longer than necessary. She couldn't help but stare at downtown in the distance to the south. This place is huge, she thought.

Ten minutes later they pulled Tom's truck into the one-car garage attached to the home of Toni Ramos. "This is where my boss lives. She and her friend will take good care of you. She'll drop you at the FBI building, early tomorrow morning. I'll be waiting for you there in the lobby."Cindi was surprised, "She, you have a she for a boss?"

"Yeah, we're a bit more enlightened here in Texas than most people give us credit for." Toni had left her car in the driveway, so that Tom could come and go under cover. It seemed like overkill, but why take chances. Once the garage door was down, Toni stepped into the doorway with a big smile on her face.

"That's your boss? She's beautiful." Tom thought about that for the first time. She was, wasn't she. And a good cop too.

"Come on in, girl. Welcome to casa Ramos. This little bit of a girl behind me is my best friend, Rhonda, we went to school together. Let her show you to your room, it's the middle one in the hall."

Cindi noticed that Toni was attractive, Rhonda too, but Toni had a Glock strapped to her shoulder, this was business.

Toni had the doors fortified and windows barred after the "Taker" incident. You would have to be driving a tank to get through the defenses. What better place for Cindi to stay? It was secure and comfortable.

Tom said, She's a good young lady." Then asked, "Anything else you need me for?"

"No, just go have a nice dinner, and I'll have her at the FBI whenever you say, tomorrow or the next day." Tom explained, saying "probably, the day after tomorrow." We've got lots going on."

"Anytime, Daniels gave me as much time off as I need."Tom backed his truck out of the garage, as Toni moved her car in to it's place.

Cindi came out of the bedroom, sitting next to the friends. Toni put a smile on everyone's face, "First thing, Cindi, listen up. My house, my rules."

"Here we go again," Rhonda moaned.

"First, you are my guest. You don't cook or clean. If I ever come to your home, you can apply the same rules to me."

"Second, my room is closest to the front. If you hear anything, wake me up, no acting brave, I've known lots of brave people who are dead, and stay away from the windows."

"Third, no smoking, inside. If you have to smoke, go outside, with me. I'd prefer you use the garage."

"Fourth, no phone calls, and no answering the phone, either. The call is not for you, almost no one knows that you're here."

"Fifth, and last, we're in San Antonio, and we're eating Mexican, tonight."

Suddenly, the door bell rang. They all looked at each other. It rang again, this time with even more urgency.

Toni looked through the shears from her bedroom, there was a UPS truck parked at the curb. She walked toward the front door and Rhonda stopped her. She stood between her friend and the door and said, "99% chance that it's legitimate. 1% chance, they want to either photograph or otherwise I.D. you to track Cindi here." They're not doing to go "Ruby Ridge" on us (where a woman and her child were shot by a sniper through a screen door.) "I'm answering the door.

Toni pulled her Glock 19, and whispered to Cindi. "Go in the hall bath. If anything happens, hit the red panic button. It's tied into my security company."

Rhonda opened the door, and was greeted by a man in a brown outfit with UPS logos on the shirt and cap. He handed her a Box, and signed Toni's name. He thanked her and hustled back to his truck.

Ronda locked the door and Toni aw the van drive away. "You expecting anything from Zappos,?" Rhonda ."

"My sandals, they're here!" Toni replied. "Come on back in she yelled through the bathroom door. The coast is clear."

"Back to my rules," (Rhonda Groaned) "Is there anything you don't understand or can't handle, and do you have any questions?"

"Yeah," Cindi said, "One, that UPS situation was a contingency you didn't cover, so I have to be alert all the time. And two, it's been a nerve racking day. Do you have a glass of wine?"

Rhonda looked at Toni, and they both burst out laughing. An embarrassed Cindi said, "Did I say something wrong?"

"No, said Toni, Rhonda and I thought you'd never ask. We hate to drink alone, but will if forced to. There's a nice Pino Grigio and a Pino Noir in the cooler. Which would you prefer?"

"Whichever is white, I'll take that." Rhonda had the bottle open in thirty seconds. "Here's to new friends," Toni toasted, and the glasses clinked.

All seemed right with the world.

Thirty Two

After a quick shower and change, Tom drove back to the Hilton. After waiting in the lobby ten minutes for Bobby Arnold, he went to the desk, flashed his badge and asked for the room which had been assigned to SAPD. The clerk gave him the passkey to room #418. Tom went up the elevators, knocked on the door, and received no answer.

With his weapon drawn, Tom entered the room, it was in shambles. Officer Arnold was slumped in the corner of the room. After quickly clearing the area Tom made two calls. The first to Toni, telling her the situation, the next to hotel security. Security was a retired officer Tom had worked with years ago, so he felt more comfortable not having to cover a rent-a-cop.

Bobby Arnold was out cold. He seemed to come out of it, but Tom had already called the paramedics, when he alerted security. In the next couple of minutes, Tom had a pretty good idea of the occurrence. Bobby's overnight suit bag was on the floor, just inside the entrance. He had been jumped, just inside the room, no time for defense. His briefcase contents were scattered throughout. The return ticket to Hattiesburg lying on the floor.

Tom checked the downed officer, a big lump on the back of the skull, the man's watch, ring, and full wallet were still there. This ruled out the robbery motive. Arnold began returning to them, but Tom held him down. "Wait, big boy, it's over, but we still need to be checked out by the medics."

"I feel like a piano was dropped on me," Bobby said. Becoming a little more lucid, he started talking. ""There was two of them, I'm sure of that. I walked in the room and there was a man with a ski mask sitting in the chair beside the bed. I forgot to look behind me, idiot! That's when the lights went out. They woke me a few times, they wanted the girl, 'where was she?', they kept asking."

"Luckily," he admitted, "I didn't know."

Tom called SAC Tillman at home from the hotel. They set a 9:00 a.m. meeting at Tillman's office, for tomorrow. "Sir, I suggest we call the other principal investigators at home tonight, on a land line from a home or pay phone." Tillman was getting the drift. "Good idea, Tom. That will still give us two hours before our witness arrives. "Are you going to call her?" Tillman asked.

"Not on your life." They could have all our home phones bugged, but the one they don't know about, is you know who's."

The next morning, Tillman, Gordon, Davis-Leigh, and Tom were rehashing the events of the previous evening.

"How did they know so quickly," Gordon asked. "They were one step ahead of us yesterday in every aspect of the case. Hell, they would have taken her out at the airport, except for the amount of witnesses around, and the beefed up security we have, now, after 9/11.

Davis-Leigh offered, "We've got a mole, an informant in the department. Someone who is constantly feeding the information to outsiders regarding itinerary, schedule, assignments...everything. This thing has to go back to Hattiesburg, Tillman said. I've worked with these agents for years, now." Tom kept quiet, until everyone stopped guessing and looked at him. "I guess this is why you have this old country boy on the case. Needless to say, I couldn't sleep last night. So I doodled."

"Doodled?" Gordon asked. Tom slipped a piece of paper to the middle of the small table.

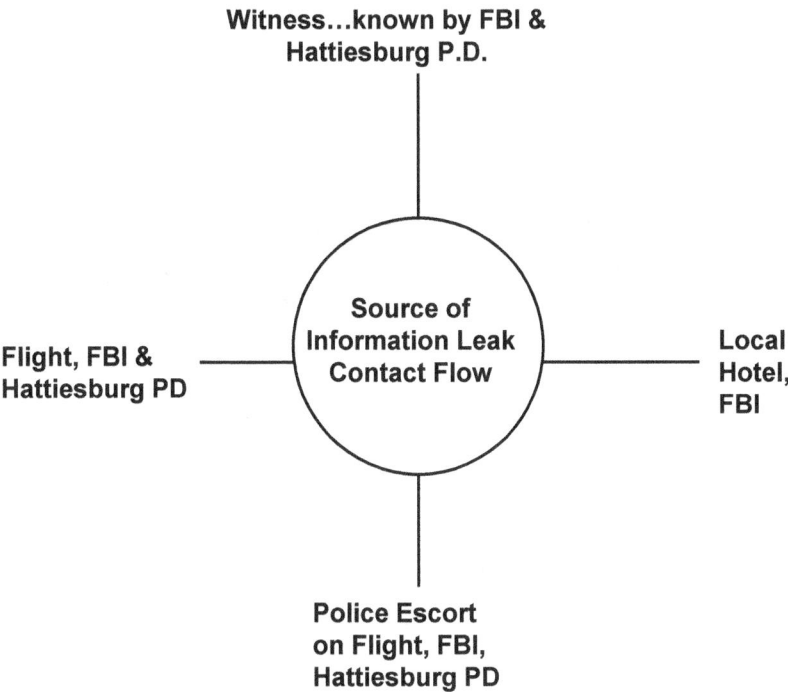

Tom, leaned forward, "Now, I ask you, did any one person have responsibility or knowledge of all these details?" They all shook their heads.

Davis-Leigh picked it up first. "We've got a bug! Probably external, we sweep this place every day. Ears in the sky, all that spook shit."

I'm just glad the 'safe house' wasn't on the chart." They all were. Only Tillman and Granger knew that Cindi was staying with Toni.

"Gordon, get me the director pronto" Timmons shouted. I'm going to ream some ass.

Tom stopped him, and asked Tillman, "Do you really want to do that, without hard evidence?"

"You bet, I'm going to have somebody's ass on this one. It's a clear cut violation of authority. You got a better idea?"

"Well," Tom began, "In Vietnam, and in all the wars before that, when they knew the enemy had broken code, or had a double agent planted, what did they do?"

The SAC froze for a second, and a big grin crossed his face. "Of course; disinformation. Feed them what they think is legit, and watch the spooks chase their tails."

Gordon lowered his voice to a low whisper. "I don't think they can hear our voices inside, we'll find out later, send out some bad info, but right now, let's go up to the POTUS room."

The group walked up the stairs to the fourth floor secure room, Gordon called and requested an agent to be posted outside the room.

They decided to work through lunch, focusing on this critical and increasingly complex case. Theories were offered, some added to a list, most were shot down. But they were narrowing down the possibilities.

Tom suggested they continue to use Cindi to get to Bayne. In doing that, perhaps they could devise a way to prove beyond question that the Agency was involved in this.

Maybe we wait for the bad guys to show. They want this Bayne fellow bad, real bad, and dead too, no testimony."

Gordon questioned this strategy. "This doesn't help us with Bayne though, does it?"

Tom thought about that for a minute. "I think it might. He's got a grudge, and anyone who thinks the CIA wants to bring Bayne in alive, is smoking weed. I'd like the chance to see us bring this to an end, let the chips fall where they may." Tom thought more about it, but offered no further opinions.

Gordon affirmed, "If the bad guys are really the CIA, it will be good that the Bureau brought them to justice. And it won't hurt our careers, either. What are they always saying during our group meetings? We need to respond more quickly and more proactively."

Davis-Leigh concurred, "All this cooperation talk from the CIA is bullshit. Ten to one, it was Agency people who were waiting for the Hattiesburg cop at the hotel."

"Let's get our ducks in a row," said Tillman. "If we're wrong, they say North Dakota is nice for both days of their Summer."

"But, and it's a big but, we have to be 100% sure of what we're dealing with, people. Let's get this briefing started, we're five minutes late, already." Everyone knew Tillman was a real stickler for promptness. "Let's see how much rope the Agency boys will give us. As strange as it may seem to you, I'm playing the bad guy." A few muffled coughs went around the room.

Thirty Three

The two CIA men had arrived in an chauffeured FBI car from the San Antonio Airport. They dropped their travel bags at he luxurious *La Mansion del Norte* hotel on the way, and arrived at the FBI building by 2:45.

Their passes were waiting for them and an agent escorted them to SAC Tillman's reception area, outside his private boardroom. Tillman went to the door, and waved the two men inside to the meeting room. It was a fairly large room which housed a round, wooden table made of recycled wood, shined brightly. Being round and recycled was definitely P.C. now. There were 6 matching chairs around the table, with water and glassed in the middle.

The two operatives introduced themselves as McShay and Reynolds.

Tillman gave them the names and positions of Gordon, Davis-Leigh, and Granger.

McShay looked flustered, and asked, "No offense, but why the local cop? This is sensitive information."

Tillman got out of his chair leaned over the table, and said, "Where I go, he goes...besides, he's the one who broke the case. Good enough?"

Reynolds tried to diffuse the situation, "As long as we're in agreement that this discussion never happened." He then proceeded to pull out a thick brown file from his briefcase. It looked like an ordinary personnel file, but was at least three times as thick. On the outside stamped in red, were the warnings:

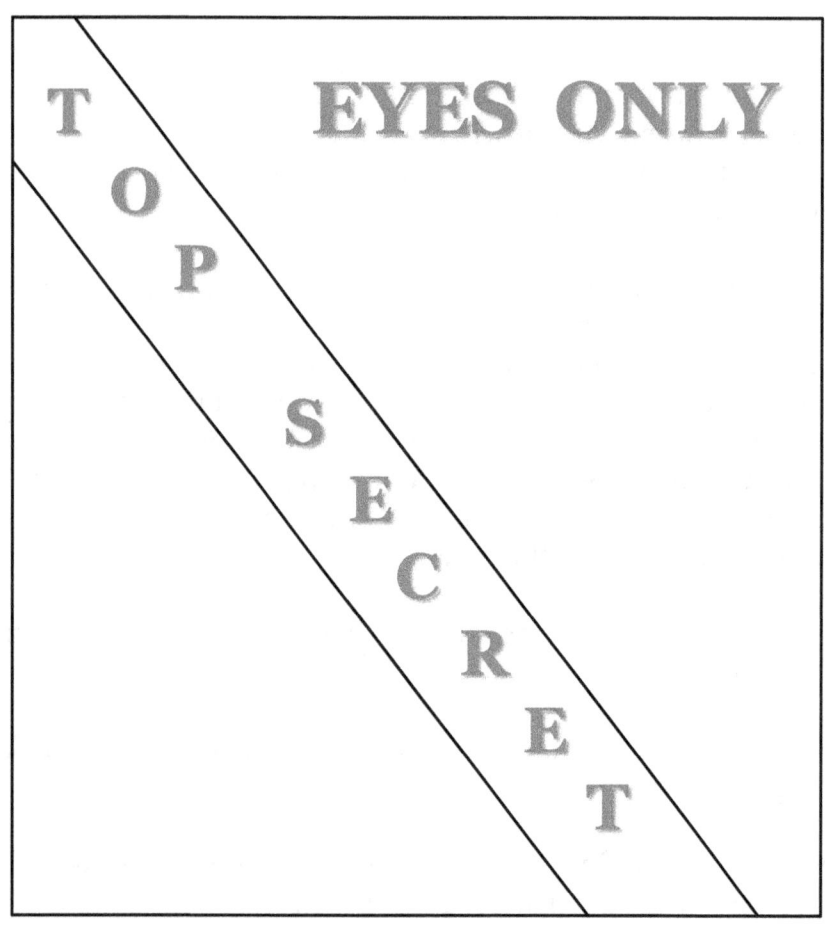

Reynolds handed the sealed file to McShay who opened the it, and noted his doing so on a "sign-in" card on the inside left cover. Tom could see from his vantage point that there were about a half dozen other "sign-ins", including three in the past week.

It appeared that the file was of recent interest to several people. Why, Tom Wondered, he guessed they were going to find out soon enough. The two men had obviously come with the "goods."

The title was "Bayne, Travis (no middle)". The first thing one would notice would be the photo. A handsome young army sergeant in full dress uniform. The hair was high and tight.

The uniform was decked in medals and ribbons. On his shoulder was the "Delta Force" patch, Special forces tag, and the rank of Sergeant First class, three chevrons up, two down. He wore proudly on his chest, the badge designating U.S. Army distinguished Service Cross, army parachutist, expert rifle award, and many others.

His assignments were listed

Basic Training: Ft. Jackson, S.C.
Jump School: Ft. Benning, Ga.
Special Forces: Ft. Bragg, N.C. 82nd Airborne.
Delta Force: Fayetteville N.C. and Virginia Beach, Va.

Operation Iraqi Freedom, Iraq.

Honorably Discharged: 15, August, 2003

Behind each of the chapters in his Army career file were evaluations, commendations, field reports, performance reviews, readiness assessments, promotion interviews, medical history, etc. The CIA men passed out three page summaries of the file, plus a 8 x 10 photo of Bayne to each attendee. The last page of the report was a medical history.

"I think you might find this helpful," Reynolds stated, but that's all we have. It showed two battlefield wounds, minor by nature, a broken finger which Bayne had set himself, and a flesh wound in the left thigh, a grazing wound with no stitched required, just antibiotics to prevent infection. McShay opened his hands as if to say, 'there it is.' But behind the main contents of the jacket were few pages in a separate file secured in thick cellophane with a small lock on it. Gordon spotted the file and questioned McShay, "What's that you're holding back," he asked pointedly.

"That's just some more, earlier childhood, background," he said dismissively. It's not pertinent." "That's bullshit," said Tillman daring him to repudiate the accusation. "If that's all it is, why is it under lock and key?"

McShay rose as if to terminate the meeting. "At any point, that's what I was allowed to discuss today. You wanted I.D., you got it. You want more, you'll have to go higher up the chain."

McShay closed the file. "Sit down." Tillman ordered. He didn't ask. The FBI man remained standing.

Tom asked the question he'd been saving. "Tell us about the ears."

The CIA men did a poor job masking their startled emotions. They blanched at the question, Reynolds was looking at the floor.

McShay recovered quickly, and evasively, "I'm not sure what you're talking about."

"We're talking about an ex-delta force soldier, an ex-CIA operative, who is out killing citizens of this country. In our days, we've tied him to possibly a dozen random murders. Show him."

Davis-Leigh removed the covering sheets from the whiteboard, containing ten crimes definitely, or probably linked to this investigation.

Tillman continued, "Gentleman, it is now 15:45 CST. On Sunday, The front page of *The San Antonio Express-News* will be filled with what's been going on, or better yet, allowed to happen, by our own CIA. Not just that he was an operative outside the U.S., most people expect that. But protecting his identity, dragging your feet, when you knew what was happening?"

"I'm no fortune teller, but I can see this being picked up by the Times, Post, Tribune., etc. I see congressional hearings, budget cutbacks, and living in a land of tundra for a couple of operatives. And what do I always say, people?" Even Granger joined in, "Shit rolls downhill," came back with a unified voice.

"Wow, he said, a story which will be loved by the Conservatives and Liberals, alike. It'll be 'viral' on the internet."

McShay didn't scare easily. "Look, one call to my boss, he calls your boss, and you'll be the one shoveling your driveway every morning, with no phone service, I might add. No way they'll allow you to pint this story."

"Which is one advantage I have, Tillman boasted." He looked at Tom Granger, who smirked, "I'm two years past retirement. And I don't answer to your boss. And leaks get out."

Tillman pointed to one of the ubiquitous surveillance cameras in the corner, "And I forgot to tell my techs to turn that darn thing off, how thoughtless of me." Looks like UTube material to me."

Thirty Four

"Enough, already," McShay blurted out, throwing up hands in mock surrender. "I need an office, one without eyes and ears. Let me see what I can do."

Tillman escorted McShay and Reynolds to an office on the 4th floor. "We call this the Presidential Suite. All the newer offices have one since 9/11." If POTUS (the President) has to stop here, he can use this room. It's lined with two inches of lead, cameras or microphones were never installed. One of my agents will be outside the door if you need anything."

While that was true, Tillman had used his prep time this morning to have a bug planted in the phone. Nothing obvious, but now they could tape both sides of the conversation.

Right now, I could use some water and a couple of aspirin. Tillman had one of his agents comply, and they left the CIA men alone. What a fucked up mess this had become.

McShay was sure of one thing that was said in the room, shit rolls downhill.

He drank some water, wiped his brow, and placed his call to the private line of his boss, Mike Riordan...praying for a voicemail. His prayers went begging as Riordan answered on the first ring..."Riordan here."

"Ron McShay on the other end here." Of course Riordan already knew that from the caller I.D.

"We've, got a situation, here McShay admitted. It looks like this Bayne has been wreaking havoc for the past two or three years. He's been up to his old tricks, ears and all, with a dozen possible actions, all seemingly random.

The FBI knows it, and the locals know it too. The lid's going to blow. Riordan leaned back in his leather chair, smiled, and said, "I've got two things to say. One, what's this 'we' have a situation Kemo Sabay? I'm not linked to Bayne in the slightest. You and your 'butt buddy' Reynolds are written all over this."

"I know nothing about that man, Senator...see how it flows off the tongue if you practice saying it enough?" McShay was sweating profusely. "What's the second think, he asked, fearing the answer, Instead, Riordan said, "We've got them right where we want them."

McShay couldn't believe his ears. "How's that?" he asked.

"First of all, give them everything. Tell the authorities down there that word has come down that the agency will cooperate fully and utilize all it's where with all to help bring this victim to justice. "

"He's simply an ex-Army killer who broke under pressure while he was in the field. It happens all the time. The fact that we utilized some of his 'Army training' is to our benefit. Then we found out exactly how unstable his psyche was, then we sent him on his way. In fact, I want you to tell them the truth. We tried to 'sanction' Bayne twice, and all we got were ears back in the mail."

"We want to cooperate, and while we can't, by law, operate our personnel inside the U.S. we can certainly provide expertise and personnel support behind the scenes."

"Tell them we're embarrassed as well. And pissed off too. We tried to handle the situation, clean up our mess, and wound up with two dead contractors. We're here to help the 'good guys'. Now go out there and sell it. And we never spoke about this. Not now, not yesterday, not ever. Just you and Reynolds beat them to Bayne, and take him out.

Just so you understand me, you and Reynolds sanction Bayne. I don't want to involve anyone else in this mess. You and Reynolds bombed that civilian target in Iraq even after Bayne had radioed you that it was clean. Now he wants to avenge your act of indiscretion. If what I've heard is true, the Feds have a girl they brought into San Antonio who Bayne befriended years ago. He trusts her. They think she can bring him in. You'd better hope she can.

You'll have a special, secure, package arrive at the San Antonio Airport tomorrow, before 5 p.m. It will be for a Mr. Diamond, which I think is an I.D. you have access to Reynolds. You two have teamed up before like this, you'll know what to do." The line went dead.

Riordan leaned back in his chair, pouring himself a much needed shot of *Belvidere* vodka.

This was getting more complicated by the hour. The harder he struggled to stay above the fray, it seemed the more involved he had become.

Thirty Five

McShay knocked on the inside of the POTUS room door and it was opened by one of the two FBI agents who were stationed there. "I'm ready to go back to my meeting down on three," he said, straightening his tie.

They went down the elevator and the lead FBI agent cracked open the door. "Mr. McShay is ready to continue, now."

Tillman waved him in. The remainder of the group had been waiting, really not able to discuss anything of importance with the CIA man Reynolds at the table with Tillman, Gordon, Davis-Leigh, and Granger.

McShay reseated himself in the same chair he had vacated only twenty minutes ago, and began his tale. "First of all, this meeting never happened. Are those cameras and mikes off?"

"Travis Bayne, beyond what you already know from his service record, was a wet-work contractor for the agency. He operated somewhat freelance for a few years after leaving Delta Force. Word was, that he had it in for the agency, and went "rogue.""

"A couple of years later we started hearing about someone who was killing, mainly in the South, using his M.O., yeah, the ears. We tried tracking him, but shit, he was the best ever. He could be Davis-Leigh over there if he wanted us to think so. He could live off the land, travel inconspicuously, blend in. We were always at least two days behind."Did you try to bring him in?" asked Gordon.

McShay thought before answering. "At first, yes. Then we tried to kill him." Looks of amazement were exchanged around the room. "Don't be such pansies, it happens, we all know it. One was a Russian contractor. Great credentials. Had done work for us before. Three weeks later, Reynolds there received Ivan's ear in the mail, at home!"

"Yes, we screwed up. Not enough talent, insufficient firepower. So we tried again, to clean up our mess. Our man in Tel Aviv called in a marker. Two Mossad agents came in last Spring."

"How did that work for you," asked Tillman.

"We doubled our results," McShay answered trying very hard to show remorse. We received two ears, delivered UPS to Langley. We were told the DNA was a match for their agents."

"As of right now, that's all we know, God's honest truth. I'm not holding anything back."

"The bottom line is that the agency is embarrassed, and pissed. I'm authorized to allow you access to all our resources, in order to bring this killer in. Reynolds and I will act as unofficial observers and advisors, only, and then only if you ask."

Riordan, back in Langley, thought things were falling into place. He was pleased.

Tillman had sat still for the entire "confession." He needed to consult with his group, privately, and decide the best course of action. He also might want to call the J. Edgar Hoover building, the headquarters of the FBI. He didn't want that, but it could be used as a stalling technique.

"I'll tell you what guys, give me a few hours to sort this out. I don't like what you told me, but it's water under the bridge. I want to use this as an opportunity to heal old wounds, but I've got to think it through. Let's meet at 9 a.m. tomorrow, right here. You two wouldn't mind a night in San Antonio would you?"

They all agreed, shook hands and the CIA duo left the building, once again chauffeured back to their hotel.

The remaining group of four hung back and after they were sure that the CIA men were out of the building, they replayed the taped telephone conversation between Riordan and McShay, which had just occurred.

Needless to say, stunned astonishment was the result. Tillman summed it up for all of them. "It looks like we've been chasing the wrong enemy. Now we've got to make it right."

He passed a note to Gordon, tell all the others involved, not on the phone or by e-mail, but personally, that they need to shut down the 'Tracker' operation.

Hint, not specifically, that it's going to another district office. Get them to pack everything except the white board. We'll store that out of sight in my office.

Tom added, "Three guesses what's in that special package arriving tomorrow, and the first two don't count."

Lyle Gordon confirmed, "Sounds to me like 'spotter-sniper' teamwork may be in play."

Tillman put his forefinger over his lips, and pointed upstairs, toward the POTUS room. They all nodded, and took the stairs. None of them really thought that their interior speech could be monitored. The building was built with just that precaution in mind. And the sweeps for listening devices were daily. But there was no use taking chances. Once they were in the secure room tempers flared,

Thirty Six

The group of four sat around a highly polished table surrounded with matching leather chairs. Assistant SAC Gordon volunteered to get the meeting underway. He had been scribbling down some ideas to share with the group, and all of those ideas were going to develop into questions and decisions.

He began, "Friends, I'm not as good at doodling as our friend here," pointing at Tom, "but here's a beginning. Something to get the conversation started." He laid out the paper he had been writing on. It was divided into four sections.

Disinformation: Phony call to emergency contact, by Cindi impersonator.

Plan: Emergency contact gives him fake Cindi's cell #. Travis calls, "Cindi" pleads for him to turn himself in, says she and Mindy will testify. "Travis" agrees, but not too easily. Says he's tired of running.

Players: Believable (to CIA) emergency contact, fake Cindi, fake Travis on phone, fake Cindi & Travis at "safe" meeting place.

Selling Our Story: Get media attention out quickly. Strongly emphasize that fugitive was trying to surrender when CIA personnel attempted to kill him to prevent testimony.

Contingencies: If the CIA team didn't show up at the meeting place, the fake Travis would be arrested, handcuffed, and brought into custody, mistaken I.D., they lost nothing, even with this failed scenario.

The group batted these ideas around for at least 30 minutes. The most crucial elements were making the phone calls from the FBI, which they knew would be monitored, making the calls believable, obtaining reasonable "stand-ins" for Travis, Cindi, and the emergency contact, plus selecting a safe location for the meeting.

Tillman had slid open a white board, concealed by the cherry paneling, and had written the four sections (not the contingencies) at the top of four columns.

Davis-Leigh commented on the set-up. "Man, everything has to go perfectly, and we all know it never does."

"That's right said Tillman, so I'm putting you in charge of finding the flaws in the plan we develop."

"Well, my first suggestion is that we give the CIA boys a quick, distant glance at either Cindi, or the fake Cindi. That way it will solidify their confidence in us, and allow them to spot her at the meeting place."

"Great idea," Gordon said enthusiastically, and Tillman wrote it on the board under the heading marked "Players."

Tom, who had been quiet, began with his usual country boy making sense, routine.

"I've got number 1, and parts of numbers 3 and 4 handled." The room quickly became as quiet as a library, all eyes and ears were on Tom.

"Folks, Slidell is the key. The Feds know he's been there, and killed people."

"I don't see how that helps us, so they know, what now?" Gordon asked.

"Hear me out before you start throwing rocks at me," Granger said. "I've got a second cousin, Claude Thibodeaux, who lives there. He would be the go-between emergency contact. The CIA might think Thibodeaux is a regular stop for this Bayne guy and even they could never connect him with me. Plus, he owes me. That piece of the problem is solved."

I've got a fake phone Travis and also a meeting Travis. He's an officer who serves under me, and is the spittin' image of this Travis Bayne. About 6'3", built solid, ex-rodeo rider. and a good cop. We put a windbreaker, hat, and sunglasses on him, and even the real Cindi couldn't tell them apart. He'd have to volunteer, of course, but I'm betting he would do it."

"I'm with you so far," Tillman said, "but how does this help us with the media?"

Tom smiled, "This fake Travis has a fiancée, Rita Estrada. She anchors the news for channel 13, KBOY TV. How do you think she's going to spin this with her boy friend involved in the takedown? We give her a three hour head start, it'll hit the entire news media within six, all based on her story."

"I've seen her," Gordon blurted out. "She's a knockout." Then he turned red and continued with, "And an aggressive reporter, too. She's going places."

"Finally," Tom said, except for a little peacetime jaunt to Germany, courtesy of Uncle Sam, I've lived here all my life. I know the place with my eyes closed. A few Sundays ago, I took my fiancée and her two daughters to the Zoo."

"We got there early, to beat the crowds. They've opened at 9 a.m., forever. To cut overhead, they changed to opening at 10, on Sundays. We set up a meet for the fake Cindi and Travis at 8 a.m., we'd have the place to ourselves for two hours. No collateral or civilian damage. They don't even let most of the animals out until 9:30."

Davis-Leigh made another comment. "There are trees everywhere for cover, but no place to hide a S.W.A.T. truck...the parking lot will be empty.

Gordon interrupted. "Ft. Sam Houston is only a mile

away. When we're certain the killers are positioned, we could start rolling from there, maybe in an Army troop transport truck, and really look inconspicuous. Those things hold lots of bodies." He looked directly at Tillman, "Especially if someone here called the Fort commander and told a little white lie about a small rumor of some terrorist activity at the zoo on Sunday."

Tillman smiled, "That could happen. We're friends."

Davis-Leigh commented, "I know I'm supposed to be the one who opposes everything, but I can help with something. I've got the perfect 'fake' Cindi."

"Please explain," said Gordon.

"We just had a transfer, actually a promotion, last week from our Jackson, Mississippi office. Her name is Jenny Little. She's the new assistant in the cybercrimes unit. She grew up in Jackson, so the speech patterns will match. She's about 5' 2", blonde, and if that fax is recent, she's a 99% look-alike. On top of that, she is rated excellent in shooting and self defense."

"Alright then, let's go see her," Gordon exclaimed. "No," said Tillman. Everyone froze. "We four go parading down there, the building will be in an uproar. There's no telling the intel the Agency could get, just from the phone calls to home." He looked at Davis-Leigh. "Angela, you call her.

Ask her if she's got 5 minutes to come up to your office. You give her the "welcome to San Antonio spiel," and Tom, who is the only one of us who has actually seen Cindi, will interrupt you with a special envelope, empty of course. You introduce them, he sizes her up. If he says

close enough, we get her back up here this afternoon."
She's the last link in the cog, as long as Tom's officer
volunteers."

Davis-Leigh called her assistant and instructed her to get
Jenny Little up to her office, for a welcome, good to meet
you speech. Nothing threatening or ominous in that
message for the spooks to fear.

Tom added, "One more thing, we're going to have to have
our own snipers in place before McShay and Reynolds
get there. They're going to look for the high ground, but
not so high that would prevent an easy, quick getaway. I
think the tallest, building there, besides the aviary is only
two or three stories, so I'm betting they'll stake out one of
those locations.

We need two guys in the trees above, just to provide
cover and flush them out. We've got to let them know
there's no way out."

"And gentlemen," Davis Leigh reminded the group, "we
can't authorize a sniper, by ourselves except in a hostage
or imminent life threatening situation."

"But I can, or probably can." Tom said quietly. He looked
at the group. "My chief is ex-marine, if there is such a
thing. During Desert Storm, he lost 3 teams of sniper-
spotter comrades. He's always blamed it on the spooks.
We'll take the highest ground, you block any escape
attempt. Our two best snipers are ex-army, Chavez and
Orlando, they'll do fine."

"Now, let's get on it," Tillman bellowed. "You each have
jobs to do. Gordon, I want an up to date model of that
zoo on my desk by 7 a.m. And I want a man and woman

to scout the place tomorrow, while holding hands. Pick someone young, it'll look more realistic. Just don't tell them why."

"Angela, go meet our new team member, it's late, but most of them work till six, the newbie's later than that. Tom, drop by Angela's office in three minutes. Tom, if she'll pass, tell Angela that I want to see her. Angela, you can bring Ms. Little with you for a surprise visit."

"Tom, then call...what am I thinking? Go by the 'safe house' tell them we won't be bringing Cindi in tomorrow as planned."

"Tell her I got called to D.C. or something, for a terrorist alert. Then get me those snipers, the fake Travis, and the contact. All without using your cell phones."

"I've got to call General Boggs at Ft. Sam Houston, from a land line. I know what kind of Scotch he drinks."

"And people, the return of the Spooks is 9 a.m. tomorrow morning. Stay off your cell, office, and home phones until we decide what we want them to know."

Thirty Seven

Five minutes later, there was a knock on Tillman's door. The agent stationed outside said, "Agents Davis-Leigh and Little to see you sir."

"Show them in, please," he requested. Along with Angela, a cute, wide-eyed young woman entered the office. She seemed, however to have an air of confidence about her. He liked that.

"I hadn't had time to meet you yet, so I was hoping you were still here and thought I'd take the opportunity."

"Nice to meet you," said Jenny Little, with a very firm handshake. "Let's us three go for a walk, I've got some files to pick up, and then you can be on your way," Tillman said, while pointing upstairs to Davis-Leigh. Jenny was puzzled, but not frightened.

They took the stairs to the POTUS room and closed the door. The SAC explained, "This is a soundproof, bug-free room all the offices have if the president has to land here and have access to 100% secure communications. That's why we're here. First of all, word of this conversation must be never mentioned. Not to your boyfriend, husband, parents, fellow agents, no one, without my direct permission, understood?"

Agent Little nodded and said a quick, "Yes sir."

We also have reason to believe that all our in-house, cell,

and home phones, plus our work and home emails, may have been compromised. Possibly our interior discussions can be heard as well, so you've been advised, correct?

Again there was a quick, "Yes sir."

"Ms. Lee, you have been chosen, partly by your record, and, to be perfectly honest, your looks, to participate in one of the largest 'sting' operations ever run by the Bureau. Don't get me wrong when I say your looks, I mean you bear an uncanny resemblance to a key witness we have in safekeeping. Bottom line, we want to keep her alive, and you will be the bait. Does that bother you?"

There was an even faster, "No sir, not at all. I can handle myself."

"So I've heard," said Tillman. "Then tomorrow morning I want you to be here, in this room, at 7 a.m. I want you to be dressed in a baseball cap, jeans, a windbreaker, and not one which says FBI on it, ditto the cap, sunglasses, and some athletic shoes. Do you have all that? I don't want anything which looks remotely new."

"I can handle the wardrobe sir, I'm a runner who always wears a cap and glasses to protect my skin."

"Good," Tillman answered. "Tomorrow morning, ASAC Gordon will tell your boss that he's reassigned you to an off-site audit, or something like that which will cover your absence for a few days. Yes, you heard right, this thing is going down quickly. So you two, get back to work."

The SAC stayed behind, picked up the secure phone, and placed a call to his friend, General Boggs, at Ft. Sam Houston.

Tom Granger drove halfway to Toni's, then stopped at a 7-11 to use their pay phone. First he called his cousin in Slidell, Claude Thibodeaux. Claude answered right away with "We don't want none."

"Claude, it's me Tom," he managed to say just before the receiver was going to be slammed into it's unit.

"Oh, Tom, I'm sorry. It's just about dinnertime, and that seems to be when all the damned telemarketers start trying to sell me something.

God-damned government left so many loopholes in the 'do not call' list that they all ignore the rules and call anyway."

Tom listened, and made a some small talk. "How's Laverne?" he asked. "The best in years," Claude replied. "No more nightmares, she's always singing or humming, she's just great."

"Glad to hear it, she's been through a rough patch." Claude agreed. "Listen up cousin, I need a favor."

"Tom, you know me, anything you need, anything I've got, it yours for the asking. You're family, and without family a man's nothing."

"Well hear me out first. It's got a little bit of danger in it. Not much but a little."

After hearing Tom's story, Claude was eager to help. "You'll get a phone call from a young girl for 'uncle C' in the next day or two. She'll ask you to get in contact with an old friend of hers, and he only trusts you with the number.

Tell her you'll relay the message. Then drive into town buy a six-pack, and come home. Call her back at the number she gives you, and tell her to expect a call the same day around 4. That's it." Claude assured him, "Good as done." The next call was to Toni Ramos. "I'll be there in ten minutes, back door, on foot. We've had a small change in plans, but it's a real break in the case."

Tom took his time, looping back and forth around Toni's neighborhood, Castle Hills, to make sure he wasn't followed.

Once satisfied, he drove two streets down from Toni's small ranch-style home and walked the rest of the way. Lots of dogs in the neighborhood he noticed. Hard to sneak up on anyone here. He walked behind a couple of houses and knocked on Toni's back door. He noticed that she had turned off the motion sensor lighting for his arrival.

Toni opened the door quickly and Tom slipped inside. She reactivated the automatic flood lights. Cindi was sitting at the dining room table, away from the windows as instructed. Tom spotted her right away, it was a good match for Little. "Hey sunshine, tired of all this thrilling police business, yet?"

"I don't know about the thrilling part yet, but I'm learning how to cook and eat Mexican food. We just finished some fajitas, there's plenty left over for you."

"Maybe in a bit, he said, right now I'm thirsty." Tom made himself at home, reaching into the refrigerator for a Corona, and sat at the table across from Cindi. Toni joined them. Tom noticed they were both having a glass of white wine.

Cindi saw him eyeing the wine and said, "Toni says it helps with the digestion, and I believe her. I think I would too." Tom replied, "But tonight it's beer only, for me. I might take you up on those fajitas after we talk some."

"There's been a little change in plan." Tom began, and immediately saw the smile on Cindi's face change into a look of concern. Quickly he grinned, wider than he felt like, "It's a very positive change, however, something which will help Travis stay out of prison, and erase part of his bad reputation."

"Now, understand, he has killed people. However we think it began because of things he was ordered to do in Iraq. And I'm not talking about Army orders, either."

Toni's head snapped toward Tom, as he continued, "That and the testimony from you and possibly your sister, should be enough to get him the medical help he needs to get well. The government will probably foot the bill, give him a new I.D., the works."

"That sounds great for Travis. So, what do I have to do?" Cindi asked. Tom said, "For now, nothing. There's a chance the men who got Travis started on this rampage want him dead, not captured. We're going to let the word out that he's willing to surrender, but only if you and I are at the surrender site. "We can't let you be a target. So we found someone, an FBI agent who is almost as pretty as you. But, I do need to borrow your cell phone." She obediently handed it over to him.

Cindi blushed, slightly. "She'll be the fake Cindi, and don't worry, we have a fake Travis also," Tom said looking at Toni. The experts think that if we can catch these two bad apples, Travis will turn himself in. It'll be all over the news, with a letter signed by the authorities guaranteeing him his rights."

Cindi asked, "Then who is the fake you?" Tom showed his best country smile, "Darlin', I'm a one of a kind. And Toni, I'm going to need your help too. Cindi, I've already said much more about this to you than was authorized," "but I felt like we owed it to you. And you can't talk about this to anyone, not even Toni, after I leave."

"Right now, I need to talk to my boss here, alone, OK." Cindi nodded, her expression showed less fear, than confusion. That was probably the best thing Tom could have hoped for at this time.

Toni wasted no time. "Cindi, don't you move an inch. Tom, you and me in the garage, now."

For five minutes Toni ranted about wanting to know the whole story. Tom stonewalled her. "I can't do it, he said, and I'm sorry to have to ask you one or two more favors, without more information."

Toni crossed her arms in front of her and said, "Ask me."

Tom looked at the garage floor. "I need you to call Chief Bernardo, at home, tonight, like right now. Without knowing the facts, I need you to tell him that this joint operation we've been working with the FBI on has turned up some real 'national security issues', and those issues are now centered in San Antonio. We need his help. We don't want the feds operating in his city on this without his permission, and we need some resources that only he can provide."

"We need him at FBI headquarters at 7:15 tomorrow. I'll be there at 7, to get his pass and I.D. He hears the story, he doesn't like it, he walks, no hard feelings."

And to answer your next question, you have to skip a link in the chain of command. We can't bring Captain Daniels into this thing, yet. This is something Daniels couldn't approve, anyway. And the fewer people who know about
it, the better chance of success we have. Oh, he'll know about the operation prior to it taking place, but if the chief turns us down, all we've done is spread the word."

"And I guess the second favor you need from me is regarding using one of my men as the fake Travis?"

Tom, looking at the garage floor again, said, "Yeah, it is. I'll ask you if you want, but I'm going to ask him to volunteer. If he says no, it's not a problem."

Toni smiled for the first time in the conversation, "Billy Cheatham will jump at the chance. And you have my permission to ask him."

Tom looked up, "How'd you know...oh never mind. He's the obvious choice. Even looks a lot like Travis."

The two cops returned to the house. Cindi was relieved that they were smiling.

"Cindi, would you mind warming up those fajitas for Detective Granger? The beans, onions, and tortillas too. Sorry Tom, we ate all the guacamole, you know it turns bad the next day."

"I'm going to my bedroom to make a quick call, I hope, and will be right back. And get the Detective another Corona, but two is his limit."

The smile Toni was wearing when she came back to the table would make the leftovers taste even better. "He'll be there at 7:15, and to make it better, he sees it as a courtesy."

Thirty Eight

At 6:45 the next morning, Tom knocked on the SAC's door. "Enter," came a booming voice. Tillman was in the office with Gordon, reviewing last minute details. Tom began, I'll give you my progress report, and it's a good one, at the meeting. But, there's something we need to discuss confidentially, and right now.

"Shoot," said Bill Tillman. Anything said to me, Lyle Gordon's privy to as well.

"Chief Bernardo of the SAPD, will be here at 7:15. I had my boss call him at home last night, without saying why. He was told that a matter of 'national security' was taking place in San Antonio. That the FBI didn't want to operate here without his knowledge.

He was also told that we need some of his resources, I didn't say snipers. If he thought we were off base, he could walk, and we'd find another way to do the job. He'll be in the lobby, looking for a pass. Knowing the chief, he'll probably be early."

Tillman didn't hesitate. He picked up his phone, looked at it strangely, and put it back down. "What's wrong?" Tom asked. "Old habits are hard to break," Tillman said. Lyle, go to the front desk, and without making a scene, arrange for a pass for Police Chief Bernardo.

After Gordon left, Tillman looked straight into Tom Granger's eyes. You've got great instincts, detective. And, more importantly, the balls to follow them.

Gordon was back in five minutes. The Chief was already with him. Tom stood, gave his regards to the chief, and left for the meeting room on four. Davis-Lee and Agent Little were there, waiting for Tillman and Gordon.

Back in the SAC's office Tillman leaned toward Chief Bernardo. "I just want you to know, Granger has the finest instincts, and is the best city cop I've ever worked beside. We'd be nowhere in this case, if it weren't for him."

Gordon added, "I agree, I wouldn't tell him that, but he's the best cop I've worked with, period, no offense Bill."

With that, Tillman gestured to the chief, "Follow me." He whispered, "The only room we know is 100% secure in this building is upstairs. I lost five pounds last week going up and down not wanting to be seen."

The SAC, ASAC, and the Chief of SAPD entered together. Chief Bernardo, I want to introduce you to the two other team members we presently have. Please excuse agent Little's wardrobe today, I ordered her to come in for a decoy project at work today."

"I think she looks fine," chief Bernardo commented. "She looks like she could take us both without breaking much of a sweat."

Tillman agreed. Then added, "I think Lyle Gordon should bring you up to speed on what's been happening the past couple of years, or moderate, at least, its complicated, and we've got less than two hours before the 'bad guys' get here."

There was a knock at the door, and an agent wheeled in the white board which had been secreted in Tillman's office.

Gordon began, "Supposedly this is a series of murders committed by a rogue CIA agent. What we know to be the truth, is that he was put on the "sanction" list by the Agency. He witnessed the bombing of a women's clinic in Iraq, after telling his two CIA superiors well beforehand that the facility was clean. There were no terrorists in the building. What we also know is that he killed three Agency assassins who were sent to kill him. These three were contractors, one Russian, two Mossad, not American citizens."

"What we believe is that this individual, admittedly unstable, is trying to flush his targets out, and exact revenge. The missing ear thing, that's his trademark."

"He mailed two ears back to Langley. The Russian's went to the home of one of his supervisors who gave the go ahead for the bombing. Their names are McShay and Reynolds."

"As fate would have it, they've both been promoted a couple of times here in the U.S. We're going to play a tape recorded yesterday. The third voice on the tape has been confirmed to be CIA Director Riordan, who McShay and Reynolds report to directly. They're going to be here at 9, today."

"Roll the tape please."

It was no easier listening to for the second time. Bernardo's first hearing made the veins in his head and neck bulge to twice their size.

"How can I help?" asked the chief. Tillman waded in, We're going to set a trap. We let them know that we have an old girl friend of Bayne's who can convince him to turn himself in. Hence the "package" which will be a sniper rifle.

I've got Army logistical help, one mile away who can cordon off the area. We'll use fakes, agent Little here is one of them, and a safe location. Once the spooks try something, we've got them."What's the location?" asked the chief.

"The zoo, Tillman answered. We set up a meet this Sunday, 7:30 or 8. The zoo doesn't open until 10. McShay and Reynolds will probably be there at 5, looking for the tallest building which allows for a quick exit. They're bringing in a model any minute, ran out of clay, they said."

"What do you need from me?" Chief Bernardo asked.

"Two sets of spotter-snipers," Tillman said. "I can't get them myself, unless there's an emergency hostage situation. Without that, I'd have to go through so many channels of people, the spooks would find out for sure."

I've seen and heard enough," Bernardo said as he rose from his chair. "I won't do that." He smiled, "But I will give you three sets. No use in taking chances. Granger can pick them out."

"Be sure they spell my name right in the newspapers. I've been waiting for some payback myself. If agent

Gordon will escort me out, I'll be out of your way before your guests arrive."

Tillman was thrilled, but got back to business quickly. "Before I forget, at 8:45, Angela and Jenny...there's a glass office across the atrium from my office. It's about 100 feet away. I want you in there, Angela taking notes, facing me, Agent Little, I want your back to us at all times, but not obviously, just don't turn around."

Tom added, "And that ball cap, tuck your hair in through the hole in the back, they won't know how long it is, and will remember it that way when they see you again."

Tillman stood, "Reports people, where are we?

Granger stood. "The contact is set. The fake Travis is picked, I'll speak to him today. I have his bosses OK, she doesn't know why, but he's 100%. I just finished writing a small script that Jenny can call with her cell number. Then I can go to SAPD and work on picking the snipers."

Gordon asked, "Her own cell number?"

Davis-Leigh interjected, "I think so. If this thing goes South, we're going to have to move her anyway. If the Agency was listening to the first conversation, they know she was in Hattiesburg. Now, they'll hear the message, between her and the fake Travis, and it will all be consistent."

Gordon summarized, "We're doing two recons on the zoo today, picking out likely positions. In fact, one person reviewing the possibilities is the head of our S.W.A.T. team. He'll know what to look for." He asked, "Tom, I'd like those snipers in place by 2 a.m. Sunday, if possible. No reason to bump into the bad guys until we're ready."

Tom said, "No problem on that. One more thing, after I get the fake Travis, we'll work on the media, but probably not till Saturday."

Tillman spoke last. "Now all I have to do is sell the Agency on the idea that we're going to work together, and that it was a tough decision to make. Angela, get Agent Little into that glass conference room, with a clean phone, and some Kleenex. We'll need a little acting.

Our guests will be herein 15 minutes. Tom, go over the script with her, I want her making the call while our friends are watching...from here, 100 feet away, of course. They'll verify that they saw her make the call, if Riordan asks. Then get downtown to you're fake Travis and get him set up for his return call. What time did you give me, 4?"

The SAC and ASAC were in place in the conference room at 9 a.m. when the two Agency men were escorted in. Hellos were exchanged. The visitors had eaten dinner at the *Little Rhein Steak House*, downtown, one of the finest places in the city.

Tillman clasped his fingers, and solemnly looked at his guests. "I've decided to give it a try," he admitted. "We've not always had the best working relationship between our two branches, but I think we have a better chance of catching this guy with you, than without."

McShay made an open-handed gesture, and asked, "How can we help?"

"Well," Tillman continued, "we've got an old friend of his who thinks she can talk him into coming in.

We meet at a safe site, and bring him in."

McShay acted startled at this, even though they had monitored the very first call from the FBI to Hattiesburg. "That's great."

Tillman continued, So even though you might not be able to help directly, we're stretched pretty thin, here.

If I could get you and your men to monitor the ingress and egress points, those being the airport here and Austin, maybe even Houston, the train and bus stations here, we may be able to nail him before he gets here,

and if he gives us the slip, catch him on his way out. We could really use the manpower."

"You've got it." said McShay, "When and where's the meeting?"

Gordon volunteered, "We'll find out soon. She's making the call at 10. She has a contact this Travis Bayne said who would always know where he was. To call him if there was an emergency, and he'd get back to her."

"She's here?" Reynolds sounded astounded.

"Show them," Tillman said, "but just a glimpse. I don't want to scare her off, not now. She's in an office with Agent Davis-Leigh. I want to be as non-threatening as possible."

Gordon walked over and cracked open the door with McShay and Tillman peering over his shoulder. "You recognize the agent, the blonde is our contact."

They looked at the back of a young blonde woman in a ball cap. On cue, she was picking opening up her cell phone. Shaking her head and wiping her eyes.

"That's enough," Tillman said, and Gordon closed the door.

McShay said the obvious, "I suppose you can monitor that call."

"In stereo, in fact, on speaker." He punched his phone and said, "Gladys, put Ms. Wheeler's call on my phone," This was an ad-lib for Tillman, but he wanted to set the hook.

The phone connected on the second ring, and a man with a husky voice said, "If you're sellin', I'm not buyin'."

Agent Little's voice was slightly quivering, boy she is good, thought Tillman. "I'm calling for Uncle "C". There was a silence for almost fifteen seconds, they worried that Claude had forgotten his lines. In actuality, it helped the sale.

"Do we have a mutual friend?" Claude asked. "We do," said Little. "My name is Cindi. Please ask my friend to call me at this number, and she read it to him, as soon as he can." Claude said, "Give me an hour, girl, and I'll call you back and tell you when he'll contact you. That is if he will." And the line went dead.

"Now we do what law enforcement people have done for centuries," Tillman said, "we wait."

Only 45 minutes later, Agent Little's phone rang. As per before, the speaker was on the call with Agent Little.

Agent Little answered, "This is Cindi."

Claude played it cool...for Claude. "Two things, girl. He'll call you at 4 o'clock your time. Second thing, we never had this discussion." The line went dead, again.

Tillman looked at the other three. We've got some time. I suggest we meet back here at 3. We've all got things to do. My duties aren't frozen in time because of this case." He looked at the CIA men, "And I'm sure yours aren't either."

McShay and Reynolds rose with Tillman. McShay saying, "We can start laying the ground work with Langley. We'll be here."

Gordon suggested, "Let's see if we can make a stealthy departure, and avoid Ms. Wheeler." The four men ducked out, saw Agent Little with her face buried in both her hands, apparently crying.

The CIA men left their passes at the front desk, and got in the Escalade McShay had rented the day before. He looked at Reynolds and said "My friend, that's progress. It's not over, but it's progress."

Reynolds was ebullient, "Let's call Riordan."

"Not yet", said the senior man. "Right now he'll ask questions we don't have the answers for, when, where, what time...no, we'll have much more after 4 o'clock. Besides, if the guy doesn't call in, we got zip, nada. You want to call Riordan with that piece of news? Me neither."

They made a call to Langley operations, and found out that their package would be in at 3:45, too late for a pre-meeting pickup, but it would be waiting for them afterward. They'd still have plenty of time, Bayne wouldn't be in today, anyway.

As arranged, Tillman and Gordon met the two female agents in the secure room, just after the CIA had left.

Tillman had never been so happy with a project. But he stressed, "We're still only half way there, but you were great," he said to Agent Little. "I just don't want to lose you to Hollywood."

"No chance of that, sir. I'm here for the duration."

His face straightened, "OK, back in character. Granger give you the scoop on time and location? Let him suggest it. You just have to be the one who reels him in. It's set, but he's going to argue, to make it real."

Thirty Nine

Tom Granger was back home, at the SAPD. In the conference room were Toni Ramos, his boss, and Billy Cheatham.

"I'm in," exclaimed Billy, the ex-rodeo rider. "I'm looking for some action." Tom stated bluntly, "I'm not looking for some hero bullshit. I need someone to make a phone call, which sounds realistic, and not too Texan, I need a southern accent, but not Texas southern. You have to let yourself be persuaded to surrender. Say you're tired of running." Toni was nodding.

"Then you have to tell her that you've been through San Antonio a couple of times, and that you'll give yourself up, only if it's to her and me. You have to set the meet for this Sunday, at the San Antonio Zoo, the petting farm entrance, it's not close to the entrance."

"What time?" Billy asked. "Tell her between 7:30 and 8 a.m. And tell her you'll be watching. Anyone else shows up, you're gone."

"Your fake name is Travis Payne. You're to call her at this number at 3:55, this afternoon. Her name is Cindi. Here's your script. Don't get too flustered, act like you're happy to hear from her after all these years."

"You'll call from here," He said, "but we're getting a 'throw-away' phone with a Beaumont cell number. The CIA knows he's headed this way."

"That's it," said Toni be in my office at 3:30, no later." Tom added, "No talking to anyone. Even Daniels doesn't know yet, but the chief does. And that TV Reporter fiancée you've got, not a peep or hint to her. We're going to give her a scoop on this one, as a favor. But if she knows too soon, an awful lot of people can get themselves killed."

Tom stood to end the meeting. "Study those lines. Repeat her name until it sounds natural. Rehearse the lines in southern, not Texan. Lieutenant Ramos will help you, you'll make the call from her office."

"Don't worry," Billy reassured them. "Both my parents were from Alabama. I can sound like that anytime I want."

"And Billy, the shot will be silenced. You won't hear anything but a ping. That's when you duck for cover."

Another bonus, Tom thought. Now, down to ballistics. Lyle Gordon had loaned him the FBI's top sniper from the San Antonio Division. He was meeting with the SAPD gunsmith, in the armory at 11:30. Tom had just enough time to get there. When he got downstairs, he heard what sounded like two old timers reliving the past.

Both were ex Navy SEALS, from Seal Team 6 in Virginia. They were whooping it up until Tom walked in. "Don't stop on account of me," he said in his unmistakable Texas accent.

Bob Dolan, the SAPD gunsmith asked, "What are the chances us two would wind up in the same room together after spending 4 ears together at 'Dam Neck?" (Which is where the team was based, Southeast Virginia Beach.)

"About the same as us two being alive at this point of our lives, I guess," the FBI man admitted.

"Detective Granger, meet Terry Adams, just about the best there is at deception, deployment, and duty. And that's saying a lot, 'cause they're all first stringers."

Tom greeted the man cordially. This time he felt like he was the outsider.

They all three sat at a small table and Tom started. "We've got a probable sniping situation. A gun is coming into the airport to be used in killing one or two American Citizens. And by the way, we've got law enforcement people portraying the targets. Tom smiled, "They volunteered, and they'll have back-up in the trees."

The biggest problem is that we have to let it play out. We can go arrest the suspects, but they'll just get a lawyer and keep their mouths shut. We've got to figure out a way for them to get caught in the act.

We've made arrangements to have at least 20 minutes with the package, before the bad guys get their hands on it. And they didn't see it when it left, so a new tape job shouldn't raise any red flags."

Dolan asked, "What do you think Terry, the ammo?" Terry replied, "That'd be smooth." We could sabotage that, no problem. He looked at Granger. "What model rifle are they bringing in?"

"I don't know," Tom admitted. "Great," Dolan said. "That narrows it down. Terry?"

"Well, the standard CIA favorite is the TL7. It fires .45 ACP, a handgun round, but deadly and accurate. Makes a hell of a wound."

"Then there's the Marine M40A3, it uses 7.62 or can be modified all the way up to a 50 caliber."

"Don't forget the Army M24. It fires a 300 Winchester Mag. or 308. Plus they could go exotic on us with a Russian VAL."

"Well, there goes the ammo angle," Dolan said. Tom had an idea, "What about the firing pin, we could screw with it or remove it altogether." Terry shook his head," Too risky, it's going to come in disassembled. If these guys are any good, they can put that weapon back together, blindfolded. They would spot that right away. They throw the weapon in a grocery store trash bin, and they on their way."

"What's the range?" the FBI man questioned. Tom admitted, "We don't know yet. Could be 200 yards. Could be 1,000."

"Is there something I'm missing here?" Terry Adams asked. "We have two professional killers, we want to catch them red-handed, and all we've got is more questions than answers."

"We know it'll be early this Sunday morning, at the zoo," Tom offered.

"That actually helps," Dolan said. "I've been there with the kids. It's all built low to the ground, natural habitat, and all that shit. But the range, there's not more than 100 yards open space, anywhere. The buildings are situated to funnel people to the different exhibits."

"How does that help?" Tom asked. "I thought the further away the targets were, the better chance we had."

"Nope," said Dolan, "the bad guys will only have time to get off one shot, before the targets take cover, and your back-up arrives. One shot, makes it easy for us."

The two ex-SEALS looked at each other and said the words, "The scope" simultaneously.

"What?" asked Tom. They won't have time to test fire the rifle. Whatever it is has been pre-sighted. We open the package, use latex gloves, brush a thin film of super glue on one side the RIS, let it dry for 60 seconds, and re-oil. That will misalign the scope by a microscopic amount, but, they'll never hit them with the first shot. Out in a field, the spotter could make the adjustment, but they probably won't have time to do that."

Tom thought that it was a solid plan. He rose to leave. "The assistant D.A., his name's Hildalgo. He'll have paperwork to get you in the back cargo rooms at the airport, and will provide for a small work room where you can have some privacy. He's meeting you at TSA headquarters at 3:00. Get it done."

Tom looked at his watch, it was 1:30 already. What a day. He walked over to Shiloh's, his table was waiting. He had called Toni this morning and asked her to invite Captain Daniels to lunch. He dialed his cell, "Lunch in ten?" He asked. "Be there in five," she answered.

Forty

Captain Don Daniels and Lieutenant Toni Ramos walked in, and headed for the table in the back where they knew Tom Granger would be. The waitress came over and took their orders, then hastened back to the kitchen. She could sense the tone at the table.

Daniels started abruptly. "Toni has filled me in what she knew of the operation, and it's damned little. I agreed to this meeting in order to do one of three things. One, I demote you back to traffic, two, I put you both in a squad car together, or three, get on board with the program. Either way, you go past me to the Chief again, and I'll have your shields."

Captain Daniels continued, "Plus, she passed me a note that said there was a possibility we might be "bugged," so here we are...shoot, I'm all ears."

Tom started. "I'm not here to defend my actions. But Toni doesn't know 10% of the story, she just trusted me." Tom handed his bosses two copies of a case synopsis he had prepared last night. It was chronological in order, up through last night, and included a photo and service record of Travis Bayne, the white board of the crimes, a paraphrased version of the taped conversation between Riordan and his agents, and a summary of the meeting with Chief Bernardo. "And I'll need these reports back, after we're done."

Daniels looked up with a blanched expression. "Is this

real?" He asked rhetorically. "The FBI is bugged?" Tom said, "They don't think it's from the inside, they CIA has access to landlines, e-mail, and cell phone towers."

Tom answered, looking from one to the other. "Let me tell you about today's events, and then you'll know the whole story." Tom explained about the phone calls between the fake Cindi and cousin Claude in Slidell, and the timing of the return call from the fake Travis. He outlined the site and timing of the sting, and the SAPD backup the Chief had authorized. They would be in the trees.

Then he told the story of how the weapon would be slightly misaligned, giving them the shooting advantage. He pointed out that FBI S.W.A.T. would come in from Ft. Sam Houston, in Army troop transports and block off the exit points.

He let them know that there would be a fake Travis, would be calling in at 4 p.m. today.

Daniels asked, "Was Cheatham hard to convince to play the role?"

Tom looked at Toni who shrugged her shoulders and said, "I didn't tell him. You hadn't met with Billy yet."

Tom laughed, "I guess you can both see right through me, but no, he was excited to be involved. It took me ten minutes to calm him down, and explain that this was a real acting job. It required no enthusiasm, he just needed to project some hesitancy and soul searching."

Toni said, It's not that we can see through you Tom, I'll bet you're a hell of a poker player. It's just that we both know Billy Cheatham."

"One more thing," Tom concluded. "Isn't there always?" Daniels asked. "We're going to give the media, and by that I mean Rita Estrada, a three hour head start on the sting. We want this story spun the right way, and she can get it started."

"And Captain, stay close, and I'll call you when the first shot is fired. The FBI would like you and several cruisers there when it goes down. They very much want this action to seem cooperative, not territorial."

Daniels responded, "Well, I guess it actually has been, hasn't it?"

The captain slid his chair back. He looked at the pair of them, with his fingers interlocked over his stomach, and admitted, "Sounds like you made all the right moves. You both have your jobs, for now, just keep me updated."

"Captain, we will, but it'll be all verbal. There may be some bugs in your office, too," Tom warned.

"Understood," Daniels said. "Tom, your punishment is to pick up the tab for lunch. And, I don't want to see it on any reimbursement requests, either."

Don and Toni left, Tom looked at his watch and realized he'd have to hustle to get with Billy for his call.

Tom paid the check and walked quickly back to SAPD and his 3:00 meeting with Cheatham. Billy was sitting in Granger's Crown Victoria, parked pacing outside the department, looking nervous.

They had determined after consulting vaguely with the I.T. and communication departments, that while the CIA may pick up the conversation, as long as they used a cell phone tower other than the one closest to the FBI, they'd never get a location pinpointed.

Tom had decided to drive ten minutes south on I37, in the opposite direction of the FBI building. Then get out and make the call from a fruit stand or convenience store so there would be some background noise. That would also put at least twenty miles between them and the FBI. No chance of picking that up.

"This is it" said Tom, as he pulled into Guerro's truck stand. Tom walked over to an old Hispanic man, sitting in the shade with his straw hat pulled down low. He handed the man five dollars and said, "My boy over there has to make a call to his mother. I'm going to listen in, make sure he tells her the truth. This is for your letting me park here for a few minutes."

The man took the money, and shook his head like he knew exactly what Tom was talking about. He said, "These kids today, they're always breaking momma's heart."

Tom walked over to Billy. "It's 4:01, you ready?"

Forty One

Everyone back at the FBI, Tillman, Gordon, and the two CIA men, were in the exact positions as earlier. Agents Davis-Leigh and Little were positioned the same in the glass office across the atrium, Little's back still to Tillman's door.

Tillman had cracked the door a bit wider, this time, just for effect. Agent Little had done so well earlier, he thought she'd sell it all the way. Her cell phone rang at 4:03, the call was also routed to the speaker into Tillman's office. He punched the button as she unfolded her phone.

"This is Cindi," she said with a quiver in her voice. Billy responded, as he normally would, "Cindi, I can't say I've had a day go by that I haven't thought of you. "How ya doin'? Are you or Tammy in some kind of trouble or somethin'?"

Agent Little went into whimpering mode. "No, Travis, it's not us. Tammy got married. They adopted a boy, named him Travis, after you. And I'm doing fine, no steady boyfriends, but no trouble either."

"It's you we're worried about. They've got your picture on all the post office walls, on the 'Top 10 Most Wanted' list. They want to get you."

"I've known that for years, Cindi, but you're right, I just started seeing the pictures posted last week. Where are you now?"

"I'm in San Antonio Texas, she replied. A local detective found out who you are. Somehow they traced you to me. He's been nice."

"They brought me here. These people say you need help. And they promise to get it for you if you surrender, and don't hurt anyone else."

"Help, my ass, Travis (Billy) said. They'll just turn me over to the Feds, and you'll never hear of Travis Bayne again." And you, they'll throw you in the gutter, forget you ever existed. Not me man, no way."

Agent Little started crying. "I got their promises in writing, right from the officials., witnessed, and everything. And Travis, the worst thing you can do is keep running. They'll catch up with you. And my life, and Tammy's won't be worth anything. Travis, you saved our lives. Let me help you."

Boy, she is good, thought both the FBI men.

"I'm tired of this so-called life," Billy said. "But do you trust me," Agent Little asked. "Yeah...Yeah I do," Billy said, but it has to be my way."

"I can get there by Saturday night, I'm not too far away. I'll give it up...God-dammit, I hate to do that. There was silence, as if he were reconsidering. I just don't know who I can trust these days. But, you sound like you've been treated fair, I guess."

"I'll turn myself in under the following conditions. I've been to San Antonio a couple of times. Once I even went to the river walk, the Mexican market and to the zoo."

"The zoo was fun. They have a petting zoo part, where the kids get to be close to the animals. It has a short fence. I'll be there at 8 a.m. Sunday morning. It'll have to be just the three of us, only. You, me, and this cop you say has been nice to you."

"I'll be watching beforehand. I see one thing out of line they'll never see Travis Bayne again, and I'll take a couple of them out with me."

"This guy handcuffs me, and we three ride in his car to the San Antonio police headquarters, where I'm booked for something minor, under a fake name. They'll add lots of other stuff later, and get the name right, they know my prints at Army records, but it won't set off a 4-alarm fire."

"I'll have a couple of days to tell my side of the story before certain bad guys get wind of my arrest. Tell these guys my terms. I'll know if they don't agree. I'll be watching."

"Oh, Travis, thank you. You won't be sorry," she said crying into the phone. And Billy hung up. Tillman looked across the building and saw his agent hugging a distraught woman, wearing a ball cap. He also saw the CIA men swallow the hook.

He rose, "We've got less than 40 hours to get this done." I'm going to play this straight, take him at his word, but we need to cut off any escape routes, and that's where you guys come in," he said looking at McShay and Reynolds.

"Trains, buses, planes, all exit points. Then he looked up, "can this guy fly a chopper?" McShay said, "Mostly Black

Hawks and Apaches, and he's good." Tillman said "Then cover all the light and commercial airports as well, That's why we need your help." Everybody know their jobs? McShay said, "Done." and they said their goodbyes.

They were escorted out. The CIA men were overcome with confidence. They jumped into the Escalade and Reynolds said, "Now we can call Riordan, but on the way to pick up our package."

"Riordan, here," came the gruff voice at the other end of McShay's call. "We guess you heard it all," he said. "Sounded good," Riordan commented.

"No said McShay, we saw her make the call, heard her on the speaker, saw her break down, and saw her hang up. We witnessed the entire event. There's no doubt, it was Bayne. We're on the way to get the package, pulling into the Airport, as we speak."

Riordan warned, "I shouldn't have to say this, but get your asses over and scout out the zoo. Find the best position to take him out from this 'petting zoo' location." McShay answered, already have the location on my car's GPS, sir, that's our next stop.

Reynolds stepped out of the illegally parked SUV, and entered the building. He found the TSA headquarters, and asked for the supervisor. "You have a package for Mr. James?"

The supervisor went to the back room and returned with a white cardboard box. He casually flipped a clipboard around to him, "Sign here, and I'll need some I.D."

Reynolds showed him a fake NSA I.D. card which read "Section Chief Pete Diamond, with his picture affixed."

Reynolds signed, and was handed his package, He turned on his heel, and was back in the SUV in less than five minutes, total. Next stop, San Antonio Zoo.

Back at FBI headquarters, Tillman's smile was spread across his face as he pointed his agents up to the protected room. As per instructions, Granger and Cheatham were to meet them there, Tillman had left a day-pass for Billy, at the front desk. They hustled up the steps to four, and presented their credentials to the posted agent.

The agent knocked on the POTUS room door and allowed Tom and Billy inside. It was almost a party scene. Tom asked, "My side sounded perfect, how did the dialog flow between them?"

"Perfect," Gordon answered, you'd believe they'd been thinking about each other for years. And, officer Cheatham, that's right, isn't it, you were outstanding, but the real acting, from agent Little, which the CIA was observing from afar, was flawless."

SAC Tillman said, agents, and gentlemen, I'm about to break policy." He went over and gave Jenny Little the biggest hug she'd ever had. If you want to bring me up on charges for that, go to it, he kidded.

"Now people," Tillman growled, "we've got to get busy. Gordon, get our two best snipers, plus the two recon teams, and any logistical personnel on duty up here,

ASAP. I want to figure out where these two jokers will be shooting from. At least the two most likely ambush positions, on the map...the map, where's the frigging map?"

"In the closet behind you, sir," replied Gordon hastily. He'd seen Bill Tillman 'worked up' about something, but nothing like this, before.

"Alright, once that's determined, Granger I need your S.W.A.T. chief here for deployment, within the hour. Where will his men be in position to provide the cleanest take down possible."

"He'll be here," promised Granger. Now that Daniels was 'in the loop' Tom could take the fifteen minute ride to SAPD and have the Captain order the man to attend.

Granger looked up to see Billy chatting it up with Agent Tammy Little. "Cheatham, we're on the clock, here. And don't forget, we're having dinner with your fiancée, tonight. Jenny gave him an odd look, and walked over to join the other agents.

"What are we missing?" Tillman asked the group. "Something's not complete."

Angela Davis-Leigh laughed. "You're missing me, that's what. The one who's supposed to be shooting holes in this plan. And there's a big one."

"Sorry Angela, we got so caught up in ourselves, we forgot to look behind the curtain, so to speak. Please explain."

She began. "The location is perfect. No civilians, close to the Army base, lots of low cover, heavily wooded, etc."

"The 'gun-smithing' idea is brilliant. From what I've heard, the thickness of a chewing gum wrapper under one side of the scope will throw the shot off by more than enough to miss our imposters."

"The S.W.A.T. teams pre-located high in the trees will ensure the assassins have time for only one attempt."

"Bringing in our guys from the Army Fort in troop transports is great."

"And best of all, the acting from these two," she said, looking at Little and Cheatham, "and the setup through Slidell," looking at Granger, "was perfect."

"So, what else is there?" asked Gordon.

"Simple, she said. What's their plan? I'm not talking about the infiltration, their weapon, the actual plan."

"The question we have to work on, is what is their method of escape? So they kill Travis," she looked over, "sorry Billy, "Now what. They have to know that Tom will be armed, and he will probably get a couple of shots off in return."

"If he has police back-up close by, his shots will signal the cruisers to move in. In that environment, with lots of low buildings and corners. One man with a handgun or shotgun is easily equal to two men with one cumbersome sniper rifle, who just missed his target. And they know 'tic-tock', time is running out."

She concluded, "One thing I'm 100% sure of, they are not, repeat, not, planning on killing Travis Bane, and surrendering. They've got a way out. What is it? That's the last link in the chain."

Tillman was stunned, but saw her objections and questions as integral parts of the operation. "Angela, I knew there was a reason you've done so well at the Bureau. You're smarter than we are."

"Let's just say we make a good team, and leave it at that," she said, graciously.

Before anyone could say more, Tom asked, "May I?" while pointing at the one secure phone in the building.

He dialed Captain Daniels office directly. Once he was on the line, Granger said, "On that thing the chief OK'd, we need two things, pronto. One, we need Chavez from S.W.A.T. over at the FBI in fifteen minutes. Two I need the head city water/sewer engineer with schematics and drawings of all lines over 24" in height, within 500, no make that 1000 yards of the zoo. We need him in your office in an hour. I'll be there, along with someone from the FBI."

Daniels replied, "I'm on it," and hung up.

Tillman asked, "That's subterranean, what about surface streets?"

Even Billy joined in. "Cars and trucks are out, I go with motorcycles. Small, agile, and quick enough to get to a stashed getaway car with fake plates. They'll need something they can change clothes in, and have room for their gear, so I'm guessing an SUV. Then on up the road to Austin, or down to Laredo, 150 miles away, and across the border."

"Good thinking, said Gordon, "we could get road blocks set up pretty quickly. In fact I'll put a plan with the state in motion today, so they can react in ten minutes. I'll make up some story about drug trafficking, and use the DEA as the bad guys."

Anyone else have any ideas...speak up, don't be shy.

Davis-Leigh offered, the Agency could set up access for them into Ft. Sam Houston. They could use their real Badges if they were on a list of people working on a terrorist threat. The Fort is directly behind the zoo.

"Looks like another call to General Boggs, and another bottle of scotch is called for," said Tillman. "I'll ask him to lock down those gates to any non-army personnel from 8 to 10 a.m.

Angela said, "What if they have G.I. clothing, dog tags and I.D.s?"

Tillman laughed, "I guess it'll be two bottles, then. Maybe he can stage an emergency gate closure drill on those entrances closest to the zoo, we'll see. It'll be completely unannounced."

"Let's go people, any other ideas, we discuss them here tomorrow at 9 a.m., in this room."

Forty Two

The next night was a pre-arranged, dinner at the home of Toni Ramos. The FBI had been in that same afternoon, sweeping for bugs. They had arrived in an "Orkin" pest control truck (pretty corny, huh?). It was meant to appear as if they were performing routine, contract maintenance. The electronic search turned up nothing in the house or phone lines.

Now was the tricky part, bringing Rita Estrada, of channel 13, into their plans. They had to trust that she wouldn't talk, hint, or break any news which could jeopardize their plan. The fact that her fiancée, Billy, was an integral part of the operation, should help, but they had to be careful.

Billy, Rita, Toni, Tom, and Cindi Wheeler were there for the meal. Toni had introduced Cindi as a friend of a friend, who was passing through on the way to Phoenix, and would be here a couple of more days.

Billy looked at Cindi and whispered to Tom, "dead ringer." Tom responded, "I agree, just don't use the word 'dead' when talking about her."

They all had a glass of wine, except Tom who had his usual Corona, no glass, no lime. Toni kept popping into the kitchen, checking on her Osso Bucco, which had been simmering just to the "perfect" stage. "Dinner's served," Toni yelled into the family room, and they all took their chairs at the dinner table, where Toni had just finished placing Caesar salad. "Wow, I love Garlic," Billy exclaimed. "I know, said Rita, boy do I know." That brought a round of laughter from around the table. They had figured out a strategy beforehand, which would let this seem less devious.

Billy said, "This is great salad. I just hope the garlic smell wears off before tomorrow's meeting with the feds." Tom stared a hole through Billy's forehead, Billy acted embarrassed, continuing to eat.

"What meeting?" Rita asked. "Tomorrow's Saturday. You're supposed to be off, with me. You said we'd go shopping in Austin, and to that petite sized store Toni's friend owns."

"Plans have changed hon," Billy said, still focusing on his salad.

Rita looked at Billy's boss, Tom. "Give it up, Tom." He played it out coolly, you'll find out soon enough. "Soon enough isn't good enough," she retorted in rhyme.

Tom looked up. "After dinner," he said, letting Rita's anticipation grow incrementally. "Wouldn't be proper to discuss at dinner. We're Toni's guests, and she's gone to a lot of trouble for her friends."

The Osso Bucco was great, served over large pasta, the meat literally falling off the bone. But there wasn't much meaningful discussion going on. Rita asked about Rhonda, then glared at Billy. Toni volunteered that Cindi would be moving to Phoenix for a possible job transfer, in the engineering field, and wanted to see some of the town before she made her final decision.

As per Toni's "house rules" she was not going to allow others to clean up. All the guests, however brought a trip into the kitchen, practically emptying the table. After five minutes, the kitchen was clean, and Rita was ready. She was sitting in the living room. Toni asked her, "Rita, would you mind spending a couple of minutes with Cindi? The police need a 5 minute meeting to determine what we can say. We'll be in the garage. Sorry, it won't take long." She smiled, "Cindi, don't let her listen at the door."

After a few minutes of fake yelling, a wall bump or two, they decided the acting had been convincing and re-entered the house, sitting in the living room.

The story had played out exactly the way they had planned. It had been pre-determined that Tom would talk about the operation, after all, he was the only one who knew all the facts.

"We've decided to trust you," Tom said dryly. If you screw us on this, you'll be covering graduations and weddings. I can promise you that there are people involved in this, who can make that happen, tomorrow. And you'll have blood on your hands for the rest of your life. And we'll expect something in return for a few hours 'scoop' on the rest of the media."

Tom asked, Do you still want to know?" Rita nodded a slow, yes.

Tom started slowly. The orphan, the escape of Cindi, who they were protecting, and her unnamed sister, the decorated army sergeant turned CIA operative, the arrogance when the drone was called in over the operative's repeated objections, killing innocent civilians.

Tom then went on to tell that this man, probably suffering from PTSS, and wracked with guilt for a bombing he disapproved of, going "Rogue", promising vengeance on those he blamed for the civilian deaths.

Yes, Tom admitted, the "Rogue" had committed murder on his "killing tour", searching for the men who bombed the birthing center. And , he would be brought to justice for those crimes.

"Now," Tom said, "it really gets interesting." Rita was all ears.

He told her how in the process of investigating the local crimes, the FBI asked for Tom's temporary assistance.

He reported that the CIA had tried to kill this former employee on at least two occasions, and was planning a third attempt soon, here in San Antonio. Of all these things, the FBI had taped, incontrovertible evidence that the killing was directly ordered by the Director of the CIA, Michael Riordan.

Rita's eyes were as big as saucers with this development. It was bigger than "Watergate."She could see it now, network anchor desk in New York, *Sixty Minutes*, The Pulitzer prize.

Tom showed Rita a piece of paper they had (supposedly) written while in the garage. We wrote this up to tell you what's going to happen, "Joint SAPD-FBI Sting Results in Capture of CIA Domestic Assassins, Director Ordered Killings."

"How would a four hour head start on this story sound to you? We give you the background, a copy of the tapes, and a copy of this soldier's personnel file." and the names and ranks of the CIA bad guys on the ground here. All before the incident. Afterward, you just have to fill in the blanks, and interview the major people involved.

"What about photos of the sting location.? She asked. Tom hesitated. "We'll try to get you and a camera man in when the operation is over, Maybe with Captain Daniels."

"Now, let me explain the why and the who in this. Chief Bernardo has authorized it, The Head of the local and regional FBI are committed. The attorney General of the U.S. has signed papers and has been recorded as far as exonerating any wrongs committed by Cindi, here, and her sister. He's promised the soldier professional help, at the government's expanse, General Boggs, at Ft. Sam Houston will be loaning us some assets."

"If something comes out of this before the operation, they're all going to be pissed off, at you. And you'll either be brought up on charges, aiding and abetting treason, carries a lot of weight these days, or you'll be in Beeville, Texas, scraping for ads to place in their weekly newspaper."

"Needless to say, we have the location, which I can't tell you, and the outline of the sting all set up. It is built on this young ex-army young man surrendering himself to Cindi and me.

We've made sure the CIA knows enough of the details to make the attempt. Then we trap them. The meeting Billy mentioned," Tom stared at Billy again, "is tomorrow. We're going to iron out the final details."

"I also want you to keep this in mind. We just put your life in danger, just by telling you this. The CIA has all our cell and home phones bugged, emails as well. Not a peep...I mean not a peep," he said, looking straight through her.

"Comprende, I understand, she said. She looked at Cindi, "Aren't you afraid? They're going to try to kill your friend, and maybe you as well."

Oh no, thought Toni, here it comes.

Cindi smiled and said, "They've found a stand in for me, An FBI agent who is supposed to look a lot like I do, at least from a distance."

Billy, of course, blurted out, "I couldn't tell them apart from 50 feet, she's perfect."

After about two seconds, a thought crept into Rita's head, as her expression changed from pity to bewilderment.

She looked back at Cindi, And, do they have a replacement for this man the CIA is trying to kill?"

"Him," she said, pointing at Billy. "But, Detective Tom will be there too."

Book Five

Forty Three

"Ok people, settle down. I need progress reports, and I need them now. We've got 23 hours to spring the trap, probably only 18 to get the snipers in position. Granger, what've you got for me?"

Tom stood. "First the good or bad news, depending on how you want to read it. According to the city engineer, and his plans there are no lines larger than 18" coming from or going to, the zoo or anywhere close by.

Apparently, there's a state restriction on mixing animal and human waste. So instead of building 48' sewage piping to carry the wastewater to a treatment plant, the animal waste is stored into a large sewage tank, on the premises. It has to be pumped twice a month."

"Now, we know the gun-smithing was done. I found out the package was delivered, to a Mr. Diamond supposedly with the NSA, about 15 minutes after our meeting broke up yesterday.

The gun experts say the weapon was a TL7, sniper model with a HT98 noise suppressor and an FX3 25x40 Leupold scope. It fires a .45 ACP, which is a handgun round, but modified for the TL7, creates a fatal wound if it hits anything more than an inch of flesh. Plus, it will throw off the forensics people, who will assume it was fired from a hand held 45. Maybe even attribute the shooting to a gang-related incident. They really admired the equipment, sorry Billy."

Tillman said, "My guys will suit you up with the best Kevlar available. Maybe we can double up in the front, and provide a headgear which would be unnoticeable under a cap, You do have a cap. Billy replied with a smirk, "Yes sir, San Antonio Spurs, or I could wear the ABRA, for good luck."

Tillman asked "What the hell is the ABRA?"

Billy grinned, The American Bull Riders Association."

Tom rolled his eyes.

Tillman said, "The Spurs would be nice. Adds some local flavor."

Tom continued, "Additionally, we have arranged to have the proper media coverage." He handed Tillman a synopsis of what they had to give and what they had to gain. Plus the headline the group had agreed to the day before.

"I can live with this," he said, handing it to Gordon, "do it, get three copies ready, then give two to Granger. I want you, Tom, to give a copy to the media contact, when the shooting stops, and a copy to Chief of Police Bernardo, today."

Tom said he would follow through, and then finished his presentation with a suggestion, "That's all I have, sir, with one extra idea. I think we need to start letting some of that disinformation out, right after this meeting. If we stay quiet, they'll know something's up. We need to plan some calls and emails, to let them think we're not hiding anything. They may have gone for this ploy, I think they did, but we can't leave one stone unturned. They're not stupid."

Gordon was next. "Here's a topological map of the complex. All the experts place the best 'kill-shot' positioning on top of the Riverview Restaurant. There was some consideration of the conservation center, but you would have to risk a shot through the aviary, which has lots of fencing, and other impediments."

"The restaurant has a hip roof which runs basically parallel with the petting zoo. The sniper and spotter could hide, early in the morning on the back side of the roof. Then, crawl to their positions, and have a flat, unobstructed view of the planned entrance. They will be firing into the sun, but they'll have filters for that."

Tillman asked, "What's the range?" Gordon replied, "400 to 600 yards. A cub scout could make that shot, if his scope was accurate."

"With this setup in mind, the SAPD teams will be located, at 2 a.m., higher in the trees in both offensive and defensive positions. Sir. The SAPD commander doesn't see the need for spotters, in a tree location. He feels that would just slow his guys down.

Position #1 will be in a flanking position, at about 2 o'clock. Position #2 will be directly behind the restaurant. As soon as the first shot is fired, #2 will shoot the CIA sniper, in the upper leg, if possible. Position #3 will be in location to provide protection for the three people at the petting zoo. I've also ordered, through Chief Bernardo, two ambulances to be nearby at 8 a.m."

"If all goes well, we'll only treat a leg wound. If something goes wrong, we'll have help nearby. I also tipped the State Police to a possible road block situation."

Zoo Map and Strategic Locations

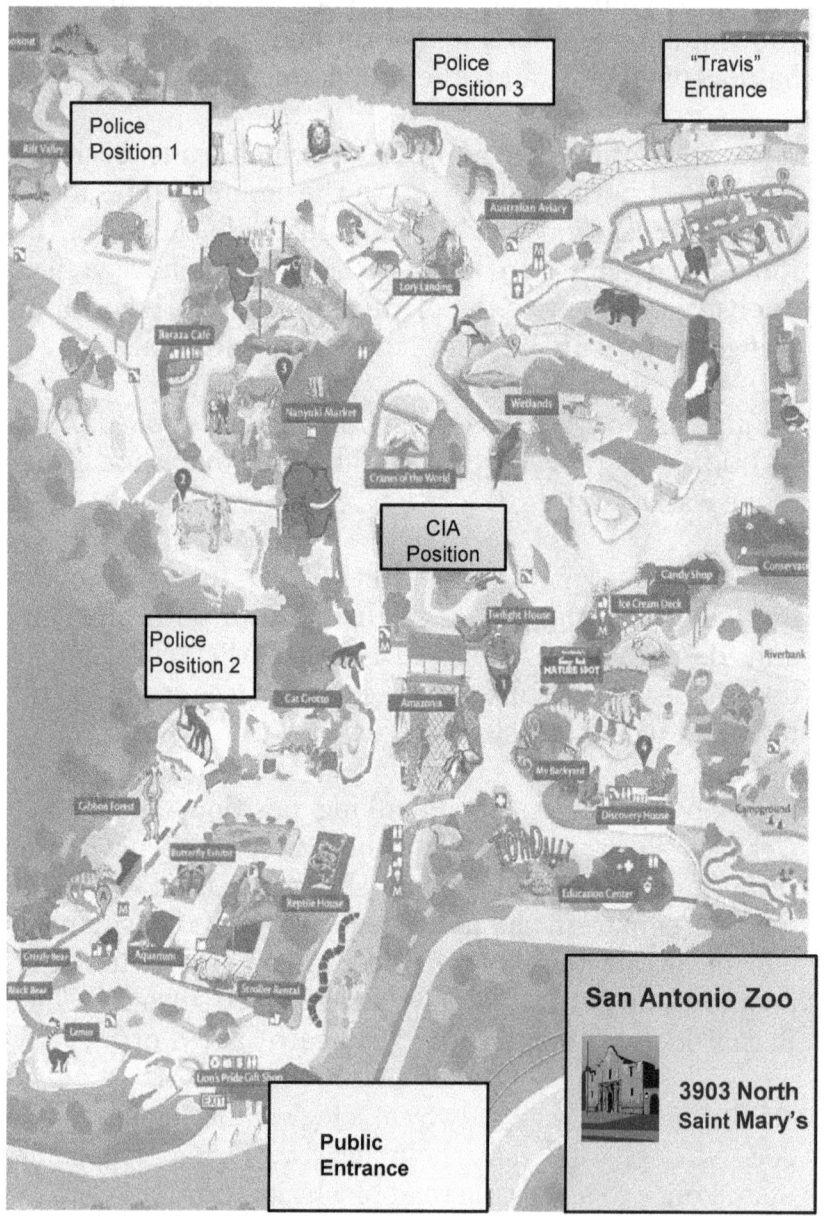

Police Position 3

"Travis" Entrance

Police Position 1

Police Position 2

CIA Position

Public Entrance

San Antonio Zoo

3903 North Saint Mary's

"I guess it's my turn, said Tillman. "General Boggs has agreed to close the gates nearest the zoo to all incoming personnel between 07:45 and 09:00...listen to me, I'm talking like him now." anyway, he's been most cooperative with us, and he doesn't have to be.

"He's also going to be at our back dock tomorrow at 02:00 to load our S.W.A.T. into the two covered transport trucks he's loaning us, and driving the team back to the base for staging."

Tillman looked at his 'gadfly'. "Angela, what are we missing? "That's just it Bill, I don't know, but there's no way they're just going with shoot, run, and get lucky. They've got an escape plan. Let's all work on it."

Tillman said, "I want two calls. Both of them in the clear, using your office phones, the spooks ill eat it up."

"Gordon, I want you to call Captain Daniels, and tell him that the FBI is playing this thing straight, no interference. But, ask him if we can set up a meeting with the parties involved, the D.A., the suspect, Granger, the Girl, all for tomorrow afternoon.

I want him booked as a 'John Doe', but I've already covered that, just remind him, it's part of the deal. Also remind him that the CIA has all the points of exit covered, that'll give them a good laugh."

"Granger, you call Angela here. Tell her she's to pick up the girl, Cindi from the Holiday Inn on the loop, route 410 at 7 a.m. I've had a room in her name there for the last few days. Agent Little, it's your job to be there in costume at that time."

"Go through the delivery entrance, flash a badge if you have to. Tom, I want you to have the 'real' Cindi delivered to my office at 6 a.m. I doubt you'll be doing much sleeping tonight, anyway.

Neither woman will be in any danger. The spooks know that if the girl isn't there, Travis won't be either, and they want Travis Bayne.

Then later this afternoon, Angela, I want you and Gordon to have a phone conversation about how you think my "hands off" plan is a mistake. That we're better equipped to handle the situation with this traitor.

"Gordon, I want you to agree, but say that 'orders are orders.'"

That should make them feel like we're holding up our end of the bargain.

Forty Four

It was 7:45 Sunday morning. The air was just starting to warm. Granger and Agent Jenny Little had parked the department's Crown Victoria, which Tom drove, just outside the zoo walls about halfway between the public entrance, and the petting zoo location. The SAPD S.W.A.T. guys were in place. They had reported two men on the roof of the Riverview Restaurant, arriving about 4:15. It was game time.

Agent Little walked in front, her blond pony tail protruding from her ball cap, wearing jeans, a sweat shirt, and New Balance running shoes. They approached the petting zoo fence. It was low, and all the animals were still in their night time living quarters. They waited for a minute or two, and Tom suggested they jump the fence. "When the shooting starts, we need to duck behind that building on the left, so being on the inside of the fence, makes it that much quicker."

Billy approached from the opposite side, through some vegetation and brush. "Jump over the fence," Tom said quietly without moving his head. About the time Billy's feet hit the ground there was a ricochet sound in the adobe fence, about 3 feet to the left of Billy. They ran to the building for cover. A shot was fired from the trees, wounding McShay in the leg. Then a bullhorn from position #1 called out, "San Antonio Police, throw down your weapons. Do it now.

At the same time Tom heard the "Whump-Whump-Whump of a helicopter. Tom looked overhead and saw a small chopper, probably an AS350, Tom thought. It was landing just outside the public entrance, exciting the animals and throwing up quite a dust storm. Two men jumped out with what appeared to be H&K sub-machine guns. One of the police snipers took one of them out before he was 10 feet from the landing area. Tom looked back at Little and Cheatham, "You two take up a defensive position, I'm going after the chopper. Tom ran back to his car, did a "K" turn and drove like a bat out of hell, avoiding trees, fences, and all other obstacles.

Reynolds was attempting to drag McShay to the aircraft, when he felt his left leg collapse from a bullet hit. Another police sniper hit. He got up, and they both struggled toward the safety of the helicopter, when a blue Crown Victoria crashed into the side of the chopper, toppling it onto it's left side the rotary blade breaking into dozens of pieces. By now, the FBI force was arriving on foot. Tom jumped out of his crashed car, and ran back to where Jenny and Billy were last seen.

Tom heard the short, 3-round 9mm bursts shooting in several directions. Good, Tom thought he hasn't found them yet. Tom heard an almost unmistakable report from Billy's Colt Python, but then a short three round burst after that. He turned the corner, and saw the man from the chopper approaching a downed Billy Cheatham. A small, blonde figure rounded the opposite corner at the same time. Agent Little stopped, raised her Beretta PX4, and hit the man with the CIA directly between the eyes, twice.

Billy was hurting, but the Kevlar saved his life. They both assisted him to one of the ambulances which were now there. He just needed bed rest. "Some bruising, but he'll be fine," said the EMT person.

So that's what we missed, Tom thought. In less than an hour, they'd have been in Mexican airspace, and then vanish. Plus, they were there to take everyone out, not just Bayne. Just then, Rita showed up with Captain Daniels and

ASAC Gordon. "All secured, sir, he told his superior, "and no good guys hurt." Gordon gave the envelope Tom had entrusted him with, to Rita.

She was all smiles. "I'm going back to channel 13, I'm calling in a remote unit. If we're lucky we can break this thing on the 11 o'clock news. That will be noon, east coast time, perfect."

By 9:30, channel 13 had a "trailer" across the bottom of the screen, "See Channel 13 News at 11 for details on the San Antonio Zoo shooting incident. The "trailer" played on a loop until 11:00. almost immediately Rita was fielding calls from the networks. Yes, she got calls from the Texas TV affiliates, and their bosses in New York. The Sunday Talk shows were chomping at the bit. The *Washington Post*, and the *New Your Times* tried to get to her. Rita's pat answer was "watch at 11," then I'll share.

The feature story was no disappointment. The screen behind Rita was a "power point" slide show. As she went through the chronology, The title never changed:

Joint SAPD-FBI Sting Results in Capture of CIA Domestic Assassins. Director Ordered Killings

She finished at 11:30, with no commercial interruptions. She ended, as promised, with a plea for Travis Bayne to turn himself in. She did this while waving statements committing the government to provide professional emotional assistance to him, if he did so. Rita was exhausted, but pleased. Her general manager came over and said that Time and Newsweek, would both be in tomorrow to interview her, and the players involved. She told her G.M. that all interviews and stories had to end with an appeal for Travis to turn himself in. The *Journal* even printed the Attorney General's letter.

Forty Five

It was Thursday, four days after the successful sting. Tom Granger was back at his desk at the SAPD, trying to catch up on the mountain of paperwork sitting on his desk. His phone rang, and Tom irritably picked it up. The desk sergeant had been instructed to put no calls through unless it was an emergency, or one of his bosses. Not knowing which, he picked it up and, somewhat tersely said, "Granger."

It was the desk sergeant. "Sorry to bother you Detective, but this guy said you'd want to take his call. Said it was about ears." Tom's face went pale. Tom quickly replied, "Put him through."

The voice on the other end of the line asked, "You know who this is?" Tom replied, "I've got a good guess his initials are T.B."

"You're correct, Mr. Granger. You're not going to be able to trace this call. I learned about 'throw-away cell phones' years ago."

Granger said, "I was hoping you'd call, so was Cindi. I've got a deal for you. No, not the government deal, although that still stands, but one between you and me."

"I'm listening," Travis said. "She wanted me to give you her cell number, here it is. The FBI's got her relocated, new name, new job, the works. I don't know where. They're afraid of Agency retaliation, until the bad apples are sorted out. She also said something which puzzles me, but she said you'd understand what she means by it."

She said if you could leave 'Lester' behind, she'd like to see you."

"I left him behind when those two scum were arrested," Travis said. I don't need him anymore." Tom was smart enough not to pry.

"So what do you want from me?"

Tom repeated, "I'd like to see you turn yourself in and get some help, from one ex-army GI to another, but that's not my decision. I expect you're going to think about the offer."

"What I want is selfish. Have you ever heard of a little town called Boerne, Texas?" Travis replied, "Small place out I-10, northwest of here?"

"That's it," Tom assured him. "Me, my wife to be, and her two daughters are moving out there later this year. If you stay on the outside, and decide not to turn yourself in, please don't come to Boerne."

"You have my word," Travis said. The next sound Tom heard was the splash of a cell phone hitting the water. The connection was lost as the phone sank to the bottom of the San Antonio River.

www.ingramcontent.com/pod-product-compliance
Lightning Source LLC
Chambersburg PA
CBHW051142030726
47504CB00004B/1000